THE

OPPOSITE

OF

INVISIBLE

The Opposite

of Invisible

Liz Gallagher

WENDY
LAMB
BOOKS

Published by Wendy Lamb Books
an imprint of Random House Children's Books
a division of Random House, Inc.
New York

Copyright © 2008 by Liz Gallagher

WENDY LAMB BOOKS and colophon are trademarks of Random House, Inc.

www.randomhouse.com/teens

Educators and librarians, for a variety of teaching tools, visit us at
www.randomhouse.com/teachers

Library of Congress Cataloging-in-Publication Data
Gallagher, Liz.
The opposite of invisible / Liz Gallagher. — 1st ed.
        p.   cm.
Summary: Artistic Seattle high school sophomore Alice decides to emerge from
her cocoon and date a football player, which causes a rift between her and
her best friend, a boy who wants to be more than just friends.
ISBN 978-0-375-84152-1 (trade) — ISBN 978-0-375-94329-4 (glb) [1. Interpersonal
relations — Fiction. 2. Dating (Social customs) — Fiction. 3. Friendship — Fiction.
4. Art — Fiction. 5. High schools — Fiction. 6. Schools — Fiction.
7. Seattle (Wash.) — Fiction.] I. Title.
PZ7.G13556Op 2008
[Fic] — dc22   2007011334

Printed in the United States of America

10 9 8 7 6 5 4 3 2 1

First Edition

To Mom and Dad

Chapter One

.
.
.

Some girls have journals. I talk to my poster.

It's Saturday afternoon and Jewel should be here soon. While I wait for him, I'm talking to the poster over my bed.

"Dove Girl, please help me."

She's a print made by Picasso in the fifties: *Le Visage de la Paix*. The face of peace. Much wished-upon by me. It's something about how comfortable she seems; calm.

"Please help me with creatures of the male persuasion," I say. "Other than Jewel."

What I want, I tell her, is a boyfriend. Maybe I won't find my soul mate. But I want handholding and kissing and I want someone to go to the Halloween Bloodbath with. Like everyone else.

Not just like everyone else, maybe. But a date. With someone who wants to be there with me. Someone I can slow-dance with, off in the shadows.

I hear the front door open, the chimes above it clinking. "Hello, Davises!" Jewel says.

My parents yell hello. Their voices boom, in a happy way.

I can't tell Jewel that I want to go to the Bath. Of course he'd go with me. But he'd say, "Alice, this is ridiculous," and "Alice, let's go rent a movie instead." And no way would we hold hands or slow-dance. Or kiss. We've been friends since we were three.

He's the only person who knows I have this habit of, like, praying to an inanimate poster. We talked about it just a few days ago. "It's healthy," he said, sharing a bag of popcorn with me in my kitchen. "You need someone to talk to."

"I have you to talk to," I said. But there's plenty that I can't share with him. "Anyway, you don't really talk to anyone else either. What's your version of the Dove Girl?"

He swallowed the last handful of popcorn. His camera was hanging from its shoulder strap. He picked it up, fiddled with the lens, and snapped a photo of me staring at him. "That."

"Hey," I say now. Jewel squeezes me hello.

He's watching my parents as they screen-print T-shirts in their headquarters for saving the world, which used to be our dining room. They're working on a new design. A plastic soda six-pack-holder-together thing is choking a tuna on the front of the shirt; on the back, the rings are being cut by scissors.

Both of my parents are in their fifties, but when I look at them now I can see exactly what they must've been like at my age. Passionate. Excitable.

Good-looking, too. My dad has blue-blue eyes and black hair spiked gray around his temples. My mom has kept her orange hair long, and the only thing that betrays her age is that now she uses those little half-glasses for reading.

Jewel's mom comes in. "Hi, Brenda," I say.

She holds up a grocery bag. "Supplies for the troops!" She's cute, younger than my parents, in a linen jumper and clogs.

Jewel's reddish brown hair matches hers. He raises his thickly lashed eyelids and flashes his hazel eyes at her. Something in Jewel is so vibrant; it's like he's in color when most of the world is sort of sepia-toned.

Mom gives Brenda a hug. "We can use all the hands we can get."

They go into the kitchen.

"Ready?"

Jewel nods.

The parents are laughing about something; Brenda teaches preschool and she usually has stories about the kids. My parents love to relive having toddlers.

I lean through the doorway. "Be back later."

Jewel and I tink the door chimes as we leave.

The sky, our Seattle sky, is gray, like it usually is, and it drips rain onto every part of us, raindrops so tiny that we hardly notice them. We've grown up here, so we're amphibians.

But we wear our hoods up.

We walk to the scone shop with the best lattes. Chunky Glasses is behind the counter; the guy looks like a fifties square, but in that way that's hip now.

The people in here always act superior because they know whether a marionberry or a raspberry goes better in a scone with an orange glaze. And they sell buttons that say things like KILL YOUR TELEVISION. But they have the best lattes. We come here, but it's strictly a to-go situation.

"Double tall vanilla," Jewel says to Chunky Glasses. "Two."

Chunky Glasses nods and makes the espresso machine swell into a frenzy of sound like a helium balloon inflating. When he presents our lattes, he says, "Lids right behind you," like he hasn't seen us a hundred times before. "And sugar."

That's an insult; no one adds sugar to this drink. He's testing our Seattle coffee sophistication.

Jewel pays, and Chunky Glasses puts our change on the counter, even though Jewel is holding his hand palm up right there.

Outside, Jewel and I drink our coffee. He gulps like a giant. I remember our first lattes, when we were twelve. We ordered triple grandes and I thought the espresso tasted like acid. I trashed mine about halfway through. Jewel drank his by clamping his lips around the cup and letting the tiniest bit through. He drank the whole thing, so slowly.

The scone shop window is covered in flyers. I notice a dog walker looking for new clients, a yoga studio beginning its next six-week Vinyasa session, and a glassblowing workshop.

"Glassblowing," I say, nodding toward the flyer. I take a step toward the window. FIRE ART GLASS STUDIO. NOW

REGISTERING FOR SATURDAY WORKSHOP. ALL LEVELS. CALL JIM. "Cool."

Jewel steps next to me. "Yeah, totally. It's eighty dollars, though."

I consider. "I still have some babysitting money from the summer. I've been saving it for something special."

"You should do it. You'd love it." His gaze lands on my face.

"What makes you think so?"

He keeps looking at me. "You want to try a new medium, right? This is perfect. I bet glass will really be your thing."

"I *have* always wanted to try it."

"Do it!" He goes over to the flyer, rips off the phone number, and hands it to me.

"We'll see." I put the scrap of paper in my pocket.

"Let's walk," Jewel says, and we head down Fremont Avenue toward Ballard.

In the window of the big junk shop on the corner, plastic skeletons dance. Jack-o'-lantern heads top scarecrow bodies. A wooden witch wearing the perfect dress—black and netty—soars across a Mylar moon.

"Holy Halloween, Batman," I say, and stop.

"Almost makes you want to go to the Bloodbath, doesn't it?" Jewel says. "If you were a cheesier type of person."

He thrusts around his latte cup like it's a pom-pom. "Go, team!" he yells.

"Rah," I say, but I'm not really concentrating because my brain has been taken over by the witch dress. "Jewel."

His gaze follows my pointing finger to the witch. "Seriously? Okay. Fun."

We take down our hoods and head inside.

The witch dress fits, except that I'm stepping on the hem. It's made of black lacy netting over a red satin lining, with a red ruffle at the hem. Curve-skimming, the fabric is clingy in a good way. The neckline is a deep V. Alluring, like lingerie from the twenties.

My eyes are sapphires. Usually, they're just your run-of-the-mill blue eyes. But not in this dress. This dress upgrades me to at least semiprecious. Some miracle is at work.

The dress was sent by my Dove Girl. I told her I want to go to the dance, and now I find something irresistible to wear. The only trick left is to get the right person, whoever that may be, to the right place to be impressed by me in the dress.

I'm so ready to show off this look. I just hope my Dove Girl comes through with a guy for me. A little romance. A dance, at least. Slow.

Okay, yeah. I know what guy I want. Simon Murphy.

Forget about him! Just enjoy looking in the mirror for a minute.

For once I'm okay with my skin being pale; it makes sense in this costume. Like I've been conjuring potions in a cave. And my hair looks fiery. I take down my ponytail, which is up so often I don't even bother to undo it to sleep.

I shake my hair like a girl in a shampoo commercial and know that, in this dress, I will not be the creepy, stringy type of witch who rides on broomsticks. I will be the beautiful kind. The temptress. The kind who knows love spells but doesn't need them.

Even Vanessa the Artiste won't come up with something better-looking than this. Of course she'll be big talk at the dance; she's always gossip, with her burgundy-striped black hair and the fake eyelashes. She gives people a lot to talk about.

She has a nose stud, and the rumor is it's actually an earring that she stabbed through her own nostril. If I got one, I'd go for a little fake diamond. Those are kind of cute.

"Alice?" Jewel says, knocking at the plywood door of the dressing room. "Lemme look!"

When I open the door, he doesn't say anything, just reaches out. He touches my hair, at the ends, lightly.

"Definitely get the dress."

I shiver, a little inner earthquake. "I definitely am getting it."

Jewel touched my hair.

He waits by the counter, talking to the salesgirl, who looks like she could be Chunky Glasses' girlfriend, except that she is much nicer than him.

"She says she'll shorten it for you for five bucks," Jewel says.

"Three inches should do it," the salesgirl says. "I was watching you. Awesome dress."

I hand her the dress. On the way out, Jewel tries on a pair of devil horns. "Not you," I say, grabbing them from his head and positioning them on a Cabbage Patch doll.

"So does this mean we're going to the Bath?" I ask as we hit the sidewalk.

"Guess so," he tells me. "You have the perfect getup. It'll probably be a riot. You might even get Halloween Queen."

"Right," I say. "Everyone will totally notice me."

"Hey," he says. "You looked really good."

He says "really good" as if he's thinking something else. The way he's been touching me.

"Well, anyway," I say, "we need to find you a costume if we're going."

"I don't need a costume," he says. "I'm invisible."

That night, we eat down at the Thai place by the bridge. We share peanut soup and each get pad Thai—Jewel's veggie, mine with chicken. We litter the table with squeezed limes.

"That show's next week," he says. "At the café by the train tracks."

When I think of Jewel, I think of him behind his camera, an old-school manual machine of a camera. His photographs are his way of seeing the world.

"Right." Jewel's photos were accepted for the show; my watercolor collection of ships in the canal was not.

"I'm bummed that your stuff won't be there," he says.

"I'll help you hang your photos." I smile at him. His work is going to brighten that café.

Jewel is the opposite of invisible to me. We're together all the time, always cracking up and talking. But, yeah, to most people at school, he's far under the radar. And I'm down there with him.

Jewel walks me home, up the hill. This area is crowded every Sunday, when the street market is open. A person can spend all morning looking at people's old treasures and new crafts for sale. Records, wedding gowns, photographs. Necklaces, candles, framed paintings. Enough things to fill a home.

Now we pass the Indian restaurant and two more Thai restaurants, patrons lingering, full of spices.

We pass John, the homeless guy. He's huddled on a bus stop bench with a can of cheap beer.

"He told me he was Jesus reincarnated the other day," I whisper to Jewel as we pass by. "He cornered me outside Caffe Ladro."

"Last time I saw him, he wished me a merry Christmas."

"Is that true?" I tap his arm.

"Totally," Jewel says. "Don't talk to him if you're alone."

I widen my eyes at Jewel. "Yes, sir."

"I'm serious. He seems harmless, but he could be sketchy."

"Jewel. He's a bum. He's definitely sketchy."

We turn and start down our street.

Jewel reaches for my arm and hooks it on his own, fancy like he's my escort. I stop at the corner and let him wrap his arms around me.

He rubs my back with his fingers, tiny circles.

My best friend, the best hugger.

I found my Dove Girl one Saturday when I was thirteen, helping my parents clear out the garage so they would have space for a T-shirt sale to raise money for endangered animals. My dad had just taken early retirement from teaching at the University of Washington. Since then, my mom hasn't worked full-time.

The amount of stuff we had heaped in the garage was unbelievable and none of it was mine, except for the rusted red pogo stick destroyed from too many nights left out in the rain. Jewel's Little League mitt was behind the garbage cans.

We mostly just moved boxes to the basement because we couldn't stand to part with anything. There were term papers in there from when my dad was in college, and stacks of lesson plans from his teaching days. And my mom's first poem, written on this flimsy paper from, like, the sixties. Cool relics, I guess.

I showed my mom the poem. She squelped. "My cherry tree poem!"

She kissed it; she actually kissed it. "Uh, that's dusty," I said.

She held it to her chest. "I'm going inside to put this in a special place."

I held up an eighties boom box. "Dad? Does this work?"

He looked up from a stack of old *Life* magazines. "I'm planning to fix that."

I put it in the basement pile.

I was going through this box of postcards that Dad wrote to Mom when he was in Barcelona studying language. He wrote messages in Catalan, which I can't read and Mom can't either.

At the bottom of the cardboard box was my Dove Girl.

Something in her eyes got to me.

Peaceful. Settled. Sure.

Her face is at rest, her lips like the top and bottom of a round heart. And instead of hair, her face is surrounded by a dove. A dove, the sign of peace.

I pulled her out of the box.

"Dad, what's this?"

"Brought that back from the Picasso museum. Actually, it's a shame for her to be in a box," he said. "Let's hang her in the downstairs bathroom."

I had another idea, so my Dove Girl has been hanging above my pillow for years now, listening to me.

It's not like I expect her to talk back.

•

•

•

Chapter Two

The bus is loud with people from my class chattering at that full-volume field-trip pitch.

I'm glad for the time out of school and the museum visit. Mr. Smith, my art workshop teacher, is so excited that the Philadelphia Museum of Art sent Marcel Duchamp's work out here, he has me kind of pumped. Too bad Jewel's class isn't part of this trip. I'm in my own little bubble today.

Mr. Smith is trying to count us. He runs his fingers through his thinning hair.

He's making sure none of us ran off to make out or to steal cigarettes, general delinquent behavior feared by the school board but probably not all that much by Mr. Smith. Of all my teachers, he's the most relaxed.

In workshop, he does his own stuff until we interrupt him with a question. Seeing him work is inspiring, or at least proof that art is worth something: when he's concentrating, he looks completely at ease. He reminds me of my Dove Girl.

I look for Clara, the girl I usually sit with in art and sometimes at lunch. Occasionally we hang out on the weekends when Jewel's off visiting his dad. She's at the back of the bus with her boyfriend, Jeremy. As per usual, these days.

They're a good fit for each other: both kind of hippies, both decent painters obsessed with surrealism. She painted a Dalí-style mural on her bedroom wall. Jeremy wears a Dalí melting clock T-shirt almost every day.

The only seat available is next to Vanessa Almond. As I sit down I feel my shoulders hunch up.

"Cool shirt," she says. I'm wearing one of my mom's designs, an oak tree in outline, with roots.

"Thanks," I mumble. That's the extent of our conversation.

Vanessa is chanting something, just loudly enough for me to hear. I stare straight ahead. This Vanessa is so different from the girl I was friends with in elementary school. We both liked to draw; we used to watch MTV together; then her parents sent her to a private middle school and we lost touch. That's when Jewel and I got so close. Becoming best friends with Jewel was so easy, like talking to myself but having myself talk back.

At the end of fifth grade, Jewel's parents got divorced and his dad moved to Bellingham. His dad was a Microsoftie who decided to do an Internet startup away from the city. He's still single, and he and Jewel's mom are even friendly when he visits at Christmas. When he left, for me it was all about my best friend kind of falling apart. Jewel was majorly freaked out by the whole thing.

I made it my sixth-grade mission to cheer him up. I'd send him little notes with nonsense jokes I made up. We acted like younger kids together; I built LEGO castles with him at his house. I taught him how to make hemp friendship bracelets.

Soon it stopped being about Jewel needing cheering up and started being about us just having the most fun together.

When Vanessa came back for high school, I barely recognized her. She'd gone from the girl I played puppies and kitties with, wearing little dresses, to this rock-star type. She wears leather miniskirts and fishnets to school. I didn't know what to say to her. Still don't, really.

She took up Zen meditation about a month ago, wearing an Om symbol on black yarn around her neck. She bent the Om from a paper clip. Right now, she's probably trying to cure the bus's chi or something. I give her another one to two weeks of dedication to the ancient practice of spirituality.

She's like Madonna at school, respected for what people think is "edgy." And also a little bit feared. No one would admit it, though. She's in the public eye like Madonna, but people are too scared or something to say she's cool. Mostly they make jokes about her style being so out there. The best part of her reputation pins her as the Queen of Goth; the worst part marks her as an outsider. Someone permanent-markered the word *freak* on her desk in homeroom.

Jewel's closer with her than I am. They're not supertight, but they are the two best artists at school, and they value each other's opinions. Plus, Jewel likes people who get pegged as freaks. They remind him of himself, or something. He had Nicolai Gregory over for dinner once, and they started to draw a comic together.

Of course, even if people think Nicolai's a freak, he's accepted. Probably because he's hilarious and nice to everyone. He's been out since eighth grade, and he's the closest match to Vanessa style-wise. He wears black eyeliner and club-kid clothes. People like him. Or are afraid of what other people would think if they acted like they didn't like him.

We file off of the bus and into the drizzle, clutching brown-bagged lunches. Mr. Smith corrals us into the lobby and pays.

Nicolai is chatting with Clara and Jeremy. He has a pink Mohawk. Tomorrow, it might be purple or blue.

I keep quiet, and so does Vanessa. She's got this bright, excited look in her eyes today. I wonder what that's about.

The first piece we see is the artist Marcel Duchamp's painting of his family. It's just a portrait. It doesn't seem like anything special, even though Mr. Smith is all excited about this collection.

"Duchamp," Mr. Smith says, "was average as a classical painter. Average at best. But he had to know how to do form so that he could disrupt form."

"Whatever," Vanessa says behind me. I can practically feel her rolling her eyes. "His ready-mades are so much more interesting."

We shuffle down the white hallway and see a painting that could be from Picasso's cubist period. It's like someone took all the cels of an animated scene and showed them at once.

Mr. Smith stands next to it, pointing out the shades of

brown and the shape of the figure in it. "Year," he says, "1912. Oil on canvas. Title: *Nude Descending a Staircase, Number 2.*"

The nude looks more like a robot to me, all shapes and no heart. Vanessa moves next to me, getting a closer look.

"The first exhibition of modern art in America happened in New York City. This piece"—Mr. Smith gestures toward *Nude*—"was utterly controversial. It was the beginning of cubism and of futurism."

Score one for me on the cubism thing.

We move on, toward something on a platform. I think it's a urinal.

"Oh my God, there it is!" Vanessa shrieks. The other museum patrons are so not choosing today to develop high esteem for the teenage population of Seattle.

Yep. A urinal. I should be grossed out. But it's pretty cool in an ironic sort of way: the most basic everyday thing, which is also totally private, out there for everyone to see. To admire. Or at least think about.

Vanessa practically skips across the room to the urinal.

"Vanessa," Mr. Smith says once we've all caught up. "You're obviously familiar with this piece. Would you like to introduce it?"

"The story goes like this," says Vanessa. She looks more like a teacher right now than Mr. Smith does. Authoritative, even with her punky hair. "Some people were putting on an art exhibit and Duchamp offered the urinal. He did it as a prank. But they didn't show it."

Mr. Smith gives us the details. "Ready-made, 1917. Title: *Fountain*."

"Totally scandalous," Vanessa says. "Totally different. I adore it."

She stands, breathing at the thing.

"Because being different," she says, and I swear she looks at me, "means being interesting. And that will always be hot."

"Hey, Clara," I say. "Jeremy."

I find them in the museum's basement lunchroom.

They haven't even opened their lunch sacks. They're too busy holding hands. I stand by their table.

"Hi," Clara says. "Sit down!"

I do, and take out my hummus and crackers. "What'd you think of the Duchamp?"

"Pretty cool," Clara says. "I liked *Nude Descending a Staircase*."

I spread some hummus with a plastic knife, smell the garlic. Nod.

"Me too," says Jeremy. "It kind of reminds me of Salvi."

"Totally."

Clara and Jeremy have a nickname for Salvador Dalí?

They get into a discussion about the Dalí museum in Barcelona, where they're planning to go this summer. "My dad was there," I tell them.

They don't seem to hear me. They go on about finding jobs to save money for the trip and I get distracted.

Vanessa and Nicolai Gregory are at a table laughing together. At least someone's having a good time.

There's a Seattle Art Museum pamphlet on the table,
so I open it. The page I open to features a piece by Dale
Chihuly: a glass hummingbird is flitting around a cherub.
They're atop something that looks like an upside-down
mushroom with a pumpkin stem.

I can't believe the detail on the hummingbird. This can
be done with glass?

"Later," I mumble to Clara and Jeremy, gathering the
rest of my lunch and heading out of the room.

"Bathroom," I say as I pass Mr. Smith.

I find the Chihuly exhibition. I read a plaque telling
me that he's from Tacoma and he's been working with
glass since the late sixties. He's a master. The collection
here is "Putti," which means *cherubs.*

I find my hummingbird. Its colors are so vibrant. Red-
orange mushroom like a sunset. Golden Putto. Absolutely
clear hummingbird. I want to call it crystal clear, until I
realize that it's maybe clearer than crystal. It's glass.

Other podiums in the small room housing the collection feature putti with other types of birds, a slug, a sea
horse, an octopus, a jellyfish, and riding on a dolphin.
They all have the mushroom cap–like orbs, in so many
colors. The only word I can think of to describe the colors
is *pure.*

Looking at them, I realize there's a whole world I want
to step into. A place away from Vanessa and away from

perfect couples, and away from school. Even away from Jewel, maybe. Toward . . . just me.

It makes the world of Mr. Smith's class, worrying about not being as good at art as Vanessa or Jewel, or as obsessed as Clara, seem so unimportant. I feel free.

I'm going to take that glassblowing workshop.

We're back at school in time for eighth period. My *clase de español* breaks into its conversation groups.

Jewel sits across the room with Vanessa and a girl named Sam, who is chewing on her blond braid. Vanessa has that excited look again as she watches Jewel. Is it possible she has a crush on him, or something? He says, in perfect Spanish, that the tree is growing eight red apples.

Vanessa winks at him. Winks.

I can't see his face.

"*Excelente,* Julian," says Señora Rodriguez as she walks between the desks. Only teachers call Jewel by his real name.

Simon Murphy, who by some miracle is in my group, tries it. "Heh. *Julian.*"

Simon's green eyes are shining. He's like one of those Greek statues, carved out of fine materials. I think of Mr. Smith introducing the pieces at the museum. Title, I think, *Secret Crush.*

Simon came to school here last year, from Portland. He was a sophomore then, but he went out with a senior girl. That means she's a college girl now. He can get a college girl. I have to stop crushing on him.

Molly, the third member of my group, is a sophomore like me. She pokes me. "I thought that guy's name was Jewel."

"It is."

I try to say to Simon telepathically, "And don't you forget it." I would never say it out loud.

Molly actually twirls her hair around her finger.

"Anyway." Simon looks at his book. I wish I didn't notice him so much. He's a football player. And he's hot. I don't like football players as a rule, but . . . he's so hot.

Our group studies the picture of an elephant in a zoo. "*Soy un animal grande y gris,*" Simon says: I am a big gray animal.

The bell rings and Señora Rodriguez bids us *adiós.* People crowd past me as Jewel walks over to my desk. He's in his navy hooded sweatshirt and ripped-up olive-colored army pants. Camouflage. He wants to blend into the lockers and desks. To be un-thought-about. He's my little chameleon.

"Friday afternoon," he says. "Is there anything sweeter?"

"Only you," I say to him, batting my eyelashes. He pats the top of my head, messing up my ponytail.

We head for the main doors of the school, not bothering to stop at our lockers. A long time ago Jewel convinced me that homework on the weekends is madness. We work hard all week and our grades keep us both in the top ten percent of our class.

Simon is standing with the football crew by the doors. Letterman jackets are their zebra stripes or giraffe spots; these guys are a herd.

Everyone but Simon has put on a dirty white baseball cap. Hats are not allowed in class. Putting them on in the hallway is what passes for rebellion among these guys. Simon has a more preppy look, clean jeans and sweaters. Black Adidas. He looks like a soccer player. Possibly even a European soccer player.

Miraculously, he waves at me as we pass. "See ya Monday, Alice." His friends ignore me, except Mike Corrigan, who widens his eyes at Simon, meaning, "Why the hell are you talking to her?"

I mimic Simon's wave.

"Why did Simon Murphy just talk to you?" Jewel wants to know.

I feel myself flush. "He's in my group in *español.*"

When your best friend is Mr. Outsider Artist, you can't go on about some cute popular guy.

The world is misting, as usual, as Jewel and I step outside. I squint into the soft raindrops and reach up to redo my ponytail. Jewel starts talking about the Bloodbath.

"It's an excuse for people to wear as little clothing as possible."

"Yeah," I say. "As if black cats and bunny rabbits run around in leotards."

"I wonder if anyone will be something cool, besides you."

"What do you think Simon Murphy will be?"

"Who cares? But if I had to guess, I'd say a vampire or a werewolf. Something that preys on the innocent. Too bad you got stuck in a conversation group with him."

That's harsh, but I nod. Jewel is clearly antipopular, and so am I. Aren't I? Simon's pretty nice. But Jewel would probably never see him that way.

We head for Green Bean, the organic coffee shop where twelve of Jewel's photos will be on the wall for the next two weeks.

Jewel nods to the guy behind the counter, who says, "Nice to see you again, man."

I buy two orange juices while Jewel puts his backpack down and pulls out his photos and a box of thumbtacks.

"High-tech." I hand him a juice. "No frames?"

"You know me," Jewel says, and swigs juice. "I'm a purist. Just the photos."

I pick up the thumbtacks and a photo of Jewel's cat, Grayfur. Grayfur is sleeping and he kind of looks like he's dead, but it's cool because you can tell he's not, really. When we were little, Jewel and I used to dress Grayfur in a cape and pretend he could fly. We dropped him from Jewel's first-floor window. He couldn't fly, but he was good at landing.

I pin the photo between two windows.

"Good," Jewel says.

We keep going. Most of the photos are shots of our neighborhood's quirks. There's one of the rocket attached to the trendy shoe store Burnt Sugar, one of the arrow pointing up by a stop sign and labeled TO THE MILKY WAY. One of the sign reading WELCOME TO FREMONT, CENTER OF THE UNIVERSE: SET YOUR WATCH BACK FIVE MINUTES.

When we're done, we walk toward my house. Traffic zooms past.

It's one of those moments when life feels really . . . real. Like, this is who I am: a girl with a fun and talented best friend, walking through her cool neighborhood. It's a nice thought, but something about it is also kind of unsettling.

"What if you got hit by a bus and you were okay but you had to stay in the hospital for months? Then who would I hang out with?"

He looks at me. "I'm glad your big concern would be loneliness if I got hit by a bus."

"You know what I mean."

"If I were in the hospital for months, you'd visit me and we'd hang out there."

"Yeah, but what if you were, like, catatonic?"

We're in front of my house now. He cocks his head at me.

"So come by around six for dinner," I say.

Jewel just stands there, looking past the tree in my front yard.

"Jewel? Six?" He keeps on standing there. Oh. "Are you being catatonic?"

He comes out of it to laugh and I punch him in the shoulder.

•

•

•

Chapter Three

After lasagna at my house that night, Jewel and I ride the bus to Charm of Hummingbirds' all-ages show. I can feel the promise of good music in the air like electricity. We wait in line in a crowd that's mostly older than us, maybe University of Washington students. "We're so good at finding teenage-zombie free zones," I say.

Jewel smirks and I know he's anticipating a night of happy, loud music. "Remember when we saw Death Cab for Cutie here?"

"Of course I do. Before they played stadium shows."

We enter the Showbox through its wide red hallway. We're immediately part of the pond of bodies, but we stay in the back where there's some breathing room. I look around and take in everything: the people drinking and laughing in the two bars, which are up a level and behind us on either side, the neon signs for the restrooms, the instruments set up for the opening act, the posters on the walls.

The light is purple. I can feel Jewel standing next to me.

The lights dim and the opening band takes the stage. The words are muffled and I can't make them out, but it doesn't matter.

The band's faces practically glow, as if all they ever want is this moment.

There's nowhere else I'd rather be.

Jewel points to the men's room sign, heads that way.

I'm alone for two songs, and the band finishes. For about three seconds, I feel awkward standing by myself. Then Simon Murphy walks up. "*Hola.*"

He's here? Alone? "*Hola,*" I say. Where's his herd? I'm so glad he saw me first, or else I probably would've stared at him all night. But here he is—talking to me!

"I can't believe I did that thing with the elephant today."

"It's okay," I tell him. "I swear, I totally couldn't remember the word for *orange.*" Which had been a problem because my picture was a basket of oranges. "So, you like the Charm?"

"Just here to pick up chicks," he says. Then he elbows me in the arm.

It's hard for me to keep my gaze away from Simon's lips. They remind me of candy. That feeling is easy enough to fight off during Spanish, but out here in the real world?

I look at his chin.

"None of my friends are really into this music. Or anything that isn't played fifty times a day on The End or whatever." He rolls his green eyes.

"That," I say, "is tragic."

"You're telling me."

"I am."

He points to his buddies, baseball caps in place, huddled together by the railing that separates the over-twenty-one area from the under. They're obviously staked out in an attempt to get beers. So why isn't he with them?

"Well, whatever," he says. "I'll hang with you, if that's okay."

Is that okay? Jewel will be here any second to find me standing with Simon. Jewel's going to think I'm insane. But how could I get rid of Simon, even if I wanted to? Maybe he's the insane one, coming over here to hang out with me. Did he see Jewel before he came over? Does he think I'm alone?

The crowd is sweaty. The music is about to start. I feel like I imagine I'd feel in the seconds before being kissed.

It's all amplified by knowing how much Jewel is not into Simon's crowd. And how much I've let him think I share his feelings. His repulsions.

I catch him standing by the bathroom door looking at me and Simon. Frozen. I hope he can't read my mind from that far away.

Charm of Hummingbirds comes onstage and everything gets loud.

Guitars, screams, drums, claps.

I am pumping my hands above my head and, before I think about it, grabbing Simon's black-sweater-clad arm.

Jewel walks toward us. I see him in my peripheral vision.

Simon screams into my ear. "Yes! My favorite song!"

I stick my mouth close to his ear to say, "Mine too!"

His hair, or something, smells like strawberries. My nose smooshes into his cheek.

Jewel comes up behind me. He puts his hand on the small of my back.

My center of gravity is off.

Simon is the opposite of Jewel. Isn't he? Jewel hails from Planet Artist/Thinker. Simon? Planet Popular? Planet Untouchable?

I try to pretend it's normal, me and Jewel standing in a crowd with Simon. I try to ignore what's going on in my body. The way I seem to be floating in the space between two very different guys.

It's the first time I've ever wished Jewel would go away.

I focus on the music and close my eyes. Test if I'll be able to memorize this scene, for thinking about later.

Things to remember: The melodic guitar music. The purple of this place. Simon's intense eyes.

Jewel puts his fingertips on my upper arms, both of them. Holding me apart from the bodies around us. From Simon.

Simon touches my arm too, sort of bumping into me, but I don't know if it's accidental.

I can feel things changing. That makes me nervous.

The photo of this moment would show me keeping my eyes firmly on Charm of Hummingbirds while Jewel stands behind me and Simon leans into me from the right.

After this show, my Dove Girl is in for some serious listening.

That is, unless Simon goes back to treating me like just a girl from Spanish class.

I've always got Jewel. But it's not like I've ever wanted to be with him, like a boyfriend. Those hugs lately, though. Those tingles and shivers. They're not just friendly.

Too soon, the show ends. People stop screaming and things die down as everyone begins to make their way out.

Simon's crowd is up ahead. They're with girls wearing orange wristbands, signs of their ability to legally purchase and consume alcohol. Mission accomplished, I guess.

They spot us, and Mike Corrigan . . . leers. His eyes are like a snake's and he looks me up and down with them. I feel like he's seeing me as something sexy. But it's creepy. Then Corrigan makes a phone out of his hand and points at Simon. Asks him to call later.

"How are you guys getting home?" Simon asks. "My dad's picking me up. He could give you a ride."

Oh. That's enough to take my mind off Corrigan being sleazy.

"We're taking the bus," Jewel says. "We like the bus. Right, Alice?"

This would be so much easier if Jewel weren't here. But that's so mean.

"Yeah. We love the twenty-eight," I say. "Thanks, though, Simon."

We get swept into the crowd heading out the doors.

"Our stop's this way," Jewel says, and heads down the street.

I linger with Simon.

"You could've spared me some time alone with my dad," says Simon. His eyes radiate. His eyelashes. "My parents are not letting up on me lately. No car tonight because they thought I'd end up driving around drunk or something."

I nod in sympathy, but really I don't know what it's like not to be trusted by your parents.

"Hey, at least I'm getting a good meal out of it tomorrow," he says. "They're taking me to brunch down at that crab place in the market. Then they're trying to convince me to hit some chick flick at the movies. One o'clock show is a discount."

"I better catch up," I say.

Simon looks right at my face, still smiling.

"Adiós," I say, and hurry to catch up with Jewel. I think about turning around and waving, but I don't. Jewel's at the corner waiting for me.

The bus is on its way down the street immediately, which is good because of the rain, actual drops. We choose seats behind the driver.

Jewel's face is red. He looks worn out, but energized at the same time, I guess from standing in a warm crowd. I wonder how I look to him.

I'm sure he's thinking about Simon.

"So." I turn to him. "Good show."

"Yeah." He's looking out the window, away from me.

"You had fun, right?"

He nods. Maybe too quickly. Maybe just because he thinks it's what I'd want.

I look out the window, see a man sleeping underneath the neon sign for a gyro shop.

"You know," Jewel says, turning his head to look at me, "that guy is totally stalking you."

"What guy?"

He blinks for longer than a blink. "Simon Murphy."

I look at Jewel and say quickly, "Whatever."

Jewel looks away from me and turns sarcastic. "He probably has clandestine photos of you taped up in his closet."

"Oh, yeah. He probably follows me around with a zoom lens." My body begins to relax. Just a little.

Jewel's got a twitch at both corners of his mouth.

"And night goggles," he says.

"And an extra cheerleader uniform so that he can make me into his dream girl."

Jewel says, "If anyone ever changes you like that, I'll . . ."

How does this sentence end?

"I'll go crazy."

My Dove Girl looks like she's either about to fall asleep or about to wake up. She's in that constant in-between state where a person can almost forget who they are. Can almost be someone else, in another world, half in a dream and half in their own bed.

Me, I'm usually wide awake.

Tonight I have a lot to tell my Dove Girl.

We went to see Charm of Hummingbirds play a show tonight and we ran into Simon Murphy.

He talked to me. We hung out. He came over and said hi and he chose to hang out with me instead of his friends. Me and Jewel. So strange.

Me, Jewel, Simon.

And Jewel was acting weird too. And not in his usual

good-weird way. He kept touching me. Like he was trying to send signals to Simon that I was his. Like he was marking his territory.

And I am his territory, aren't I? To put it severely. Not his girlfriend. But I'm his more than anyone else's. It should be fine with me if he touches me in front of Simon Murphy.

But I'm still not sure if I like Simon seeing me claimed by Jewel, or this new aspect of Jewel that makes him feel the need to do that.

Simon . . . who knew? We share the same taste in music, and he's not as tight with the elite crowd as I thought.

Dove Girl, I really want to see him outside school again. On our own.

And I have a plan for how to do that.

•

•

•

Chapter Four

Saturday morning, a little groggy from not a whole lot of sleep, I wake to the smell of bacon cooking. I shower quickly and drag on my jeans, stripy sweater, and Pumas. Put my hair in a ponytail. I am uniformed.

When I get downstairs, Mom is cracking eggs and Dad is reading the paper, standing by the coffeemaker, waiting for the brew.

"Scrambled?" Mom asks.

"Of course."

I sit down at the table in our diner-style kitchen. The walls are painted red and covered in Coca-Cola memorabilia: a clock in the shape of a bottle, a tin advertisement featuring a smiling girl with bows in her hair, a poster of teenagers sharing their drink from two straws in one tall glass. My parents bought the stuff before they started being all organic, all the time.

"To stunt your growth," Dad says as he puts down my coffee. A joke. I am pretty well developed for a fifteen-year-old.

He goes back to the counter and retrieves his own plate. Mom has arranged his sunny-side-up eggs like eyes with a bacon smile. Cute.

He sits with me. We eat.

"Your mom and I want to go by that coffee shop to see Jewel's photo show," he says. "You submitted pieces too, didn't you?"

"Didn't make the cut. I did help Jewel, though. Maybe behind every great artist, there's a girl who knows how to hang pictures."

"Alice," my dad says. "Your drawings are getting better all the time."

"Not really, Dad. But thanks."

He does know what he's talking about when it comes to art, but my dad would say nice things to me even if he knew I sucked. Which makes it hard to tell what he thinks sometimes.

Jewel is an artistic genius. Of course only a certain type of person bothers to notice his amazing talent. I get some credibility around the art workshop just for being his friend. Even Mr. Smith seems to think I'm better than I am.

I don't want to be the hey-is-this-hanging-straight girl forever.

"My glassblowing workshop is next weekend," I say.

"Looking forward to it?" Dad asks.

"Yep."

We finish breakfast and Dad heads out to the driveway, where he spends the bulk of every weekend working on his vintage Chevy.

Sometimes I help him, which mostly means handing him tools. But not today.

∾

My parents and I have been out of the Pike Place Market spice tea for two weeks, so it's a good excuse to go down to the market. I tell myself that this is not a decision to accidentally-on-purpose run into Simon Murphy. And that I'm not inviting Jewel for his own good, because he hates crowds.

I look in my mom's full-length mirror before leaving. My usual: ponytail, lip gloss, sweater, jeans. But are my jeans shorter now? Definitely, I'm taller. I thought this was supposed to happen when you're nine, not fifteen. But there it is. Growth spurt. Long legs are a definite improvement, right?

I put on my blue corduroy jacket and head out. I take the 26 bus downtown, get off by Nordstrom Rack. I think about checking out their cheap sneakers, decide against it, and walk down one steep block to the market. The city is gray, as usual, and I can smell salt from the sound; the water is as gray as the sky.

The market, with its giant red neon sign, is always crowded. But I like to take it all in, especially now, in the fall, when sunflowers and dahlias bloom and I can look at them clustered together in metal buckets just waiting to be bought, smiles you can take home.

This place always makes me feel like I'm French or something, like I should be wearing a bonnet as I buy the week's sheep innards. Definitely like I'm not me. Not a regular girl.

When I asked my Dove Girl for a boyfriend, I was not

expecting anyone like Simon Murphy. Simon can't be my wish come true. It would throw the whole social stratum out of whack. I'm nobody but Jewel's friend. And that's only to the people who bother to notice Jewel.

The nonartist types who do notice him tend to think he's gay. It's been a common misconception among the baseball-hat crew ever since middle school. Because Jewel's best friend is a girl, I guess. And because he's creative.

Probably most of our class doesn't know either one of our names, let alone anything else about us. Invisible. For me to go out with Simon would be school-paper-headline-worthy news. Okay, it might not be quite that big of a deal. Simon's not *totally* the most popular guy in school—that's Mike Corrigan.

The tea shop is full of big jars of loose tea to buy in bulk. I take the lid off the orange spice blend, move my nose to the rim of the jar, close my eyes, and inhale. India. The painting of this tea would be dark orange and some shade of purple. The shape would be vaguely lotus flower.

I buy the Market Spice and then I wander, keeping my jacket pulled tightly over my sweater. Some of the sunflowers are so tall. They look like really skinny people with lollipop-proportioned heads. Smiling at their own crazy hair. The dahlias are my favorite, though. Such bright pinks and oranges. So many petals. Like the orange spice tea, the dahlias make me feel like I've traveled to other places, even to other times.

I stand at the fish and chips counter near the leather goods stall, deciding whether I'm hungry. It's so weird, the power of place. I don't have to try hard to imagine I'm on another planet. Like fish and chips are food for aliens. Because how can so many sensations exist so close to home—the smell of salt water, fish ready to be cooked, the fainter scent of sweet fruit, the colors of everything, the voices of the people, the drum of KEXP playing in the background.

Simon came for brunch, and his family needs time to make it up to Pacific Place for a one o'clock movie. The timing should be perfect, and the crab place is just past the vendors. To get out of the market, he'll have to pass this way.

I sit at the fish and chips counter.

There he is.

Simon is at the leather stall trying on cuff bracelets. His head is down, the same tilt as when he looks at his Spanish book. I can't go over there. I manage to not stare at him as I order fries and soda. It takes all my effort to casually study the intricacies of the linoleum countertop.

Simon taps my shoulder. He's got on his backpack and he's wearing a tightish turquoise sweater under his bright green Adidas vest, and very well-faded jeans, possibly so well faded that the fading was done prepurchase. His chocolate-colored hair is messy but the look is styled. Lots of gel. I evaluate him like he's some guy in a magazine.

"I keep running into you this weekend," he says.

"Yeah, I noticed." I hear Jewel's voice in my head. "*That guy is totally stalking you.*" I hope Simon doesn't think I'm stalking him. Especially since I kind of am.

"Do you come downtown a lot?" he asks.

"I like to," I say. "It feels like a vacation."

Oh, no. That was probably a really weird thing to say. What wouldn't I do for the time-rewind superpower?

"Yeah, I know what you mean," he says. "There's a lot of stuff to do."

Phew. "Yep."

"I volunteer at the aquarium."

"That's so cool!"

"I even get to feed the octopus." He grins like he just won the Super Bowl.

"No way." The fish and chips guy gives me my food. Simon sits on the stool next to mine.

"I'm meeting my parents later. They're at the movies now, up at Pacific Place, but it was nothing I wanted to see." He looks up at the chalkboard menu.

"Oh," I say, and take a sip of my soda. Brilliant conversation.

"I was gonna do that Spanish sheet as proof of my ability to study in public. Maybe get a candy apple, too. Does brunch have dessert?"

"Any meal can have dessert, as far as I'm concerned. I love that candy apple place," I say. "Actually, I just like looking in the window. But I've always wanted to try it out."

"I'll wait while you eat so you can go with me."

Simon sips a Coke while I try to eat my fries. I offer him some.

"Thanks." He grabs a five-fry pinch.

"So," I say. "Tell me about the octopus."

"We feed her crab bits inside Mr. Potato Head."

I can't help chuckling at the thought. "The toy?"

"Yeah. You know, Mr. Potato Head has that hatch for his eyes and nose and stuff? We put the food in there and close the hatch. It's fun for people to watch her play with it. Only takes a minute for her to get it open."

"So it's a girl octopus?"

He nods. "Oh, yeah. Sad thing, though. They mated her. She'll lay eggs soon."

"That sounds happy."

"Not for her. She won't eat while she's taking care of the eggs. When they hatch, she'll die."

I drop my fry. "That's horrible!"

"Yeah. But it's natural for the octopus."

So cool that Simon knows this stuff.

"Let's talk about something else," he says.

I hate when people say that. "Um."

"The show was good last night." That, I can talk about. "Robb Moore is a genius."

"I know, how can you not love the Charm?" I sip my Coke.

"I wouldn't know."

He takes another bunch of my fries. He finishes chewing and says, "What's with your friend, anyway? He is just your friend, right?"

I take the soda straw from my lips. "Yes." Did that sound too formal? "Yeah."

" 'Cause he's the only person I ever see you talking to. Practically."

"We're good friends."

"Is he gay?"

Personal, personal. At this point, though, I don't care; if he's interested in who I'm dating, and who I'm not, he can say anything he wants. Like I've ever even been on a date.

"Jewel is definitely not gay."

"He's just . . . you know. So different."

"He's an artist. He's really talented."

"Yeah?" Simon says. "You know him a lot better than I do."

"And you know everyone else in school a lot better than I do."

Simon eats some fries. "Why are you so quiet at school?"

I certainly don't announce my comings and goings like the how-was-your-weekend homeroom crowd. But I'm not a mouse. Unless. Unless that's exactly what I am. Mousy. Boring. Ordinary. A little timid. Easy to miss if not in a state of scamper.

I keep eating my fries.

"You should talk more," Simon says. "If you showed up to one of our parties and asked for a beer, everyone would love you."

Gee. Just what I want. The love of keg kids.

But really. I study my plate, then sneak a look at Simon. Maybe the secret to having a lot of friends in high school isn't a secret at all. Maybe it's all about being in the right place at the right time. With the right person.

∾

The candy apple shop is right near the original location of Starbucks, the only one to still feature the mermaid logo in all her bare-breasted glory. Apples line the windows: coated in red, in caramel, in chocolate, and in any topping you can imagine, from nuts to sprinkles to full-on candy chunks.

"The one with M&M's and chocolate is my favorite," says Simon.

"That's some heavy-duty apple eating."

He puffs out his chest. "I can handle it."

Is he being sarcastic? God, I hope he is, with that macho thing. Tarzan is so not my style. All those grunts. The loincloth.

How about . . . we are candy-apple Adam and Eve. Tempted.

The loincloth imagery is quite strong for me at the moment. But Adam would have been totally naked.

I so should not be thinking about that.

Being around Simon has got me feeling something tingly in my throat. I want so badly to nuzzle against his neck, my lips against his skin.

Stop! Stop lusting after him.

I choose a plain caramel apple and Simon gets his favorite.

"My treat," he says, and pays before I can protest.

We sit on a bench next to a huge stuffed teddy bear.

Simon asks me what I think of Spanish class. "For real," he says, "does Señora's accent ever crack you up?"

Our teacher is from El Salvador. "Crack me up? No. She speaks English better than I'll ever speak Spanish."

"I knew you'd say something like that. Something fair."

"I guess."

"My friends say she should be washing their sheets."

I sit up. "What! That's horrible. Cruel. Your friends are mean."

"Yeah," he says. "They kind of are."

"Sorry to say that, but I mean, that's really terrible."

"I know. It's okay. I've always figured that you and Jewel kind of hate us."

I look at my lap. "Not *you*."

"Jewel does. He was . . . glaring at me at the show."

Well. "He doesn't know you."

He looks right at me. "There's a lot you don't know about me."

"There's a lot you don't know about Jewel. And about me."

"I'm sure there is." He has a little bit of green M&M shell on his bottom lip. "You know, I only moved to Seattle last year. Most of my friends then were seniors 'cause I made varsity football. Now they're off at school. I don't really know anyone here that well."

I know he dated a senior cheerleader last year. She was on the homecoming court. "You seem to do all right."

"I'm outgoing, I guess."

"Yeah," I say, and concentrate on biting my apple.

"Honestly?" He stops eating again but stares at his apple. He's about to say something big. "I don't really care about football and all that. But it's fun. The parties and everything." He turns his eyes back to his apple.

"But . . ."

"I'm kinda done with the whole thing. It's fun but it's not . . . I don't know. It's not enough? To define me? All the time?"

I know that popularity doesn't buy happiness, but I can't help thinking it might make things easier. "Okay," I say. I guess what I'm thinking is *At least you get to have fun. At least you have more than one real friend.*

Then again, it's kind of like what he's saying is *I don't have any real friends. Just fun people.*

"How does our school compare to your old one?"

"Same old," he says. "Cliques. The outsider types here have taken it to kind of a new level, though. Like Vanessa Almond and that guy Nicolai? They're out there."

Like me? I wonder. Not my look, but I'm in that art crowd.

"I like it, though," he continues. "They really know who they are. Or they at least think they do. It's kind of . . . brave."

"To dress like a freak?"

"To be who you are. In high school."

Simon finishes his apple and gets up to throw away the stick. "Come on," he says. "Let's walk."

"It's not weird," I tell Simon as we move to a bench on the stretch of grass down by the water near the market.

"What's not weird?"

"Talking to you," I say. "Even though we've never

really talked before." I can't believe I'm saying this stuff to him.

I sweep my hand out to indicate the park, the bay, the homeless people gathered in a clump.

I'm feeling brave now. "Why did you even come up to me back there, at the lunch counter?"

He looks at me.

He keeps looking at me. With those eyes.

Then he does something amazing. Puts his fingers under my chin.

Simon Murphy, whose perfect girl had to be a cheerleader. That's what I thought. That's what Jewel and I joked about.

He kisses me. He kisses me with candy still on his lips. So quickly I'm not sure it really was a kiss.

If it was, it was my first.

My heart is trying to beat itself out of my chest. I hope he can't feel it. I hope he can. My toes are bent up in my shoes.

Then he kisses me again, for real. This is easy; is this too easy? Why is he doing this? Does it matter?

I try to melt into him. I try not to worry about my chest exploding as my heart pumps too fast. I try to remember what I've read in magazines about kissing. Open my mouth a little. Let him in.

Just as he pulls away, I think *People are watching this; they think we're a couple.*

People would believe that this guy is with me.

"Why wouldn't I come up to you?" he asks.

It takes a moment for me to remember what we'd been talking about.

I don't know how to answer that without saying, "Why *would* you?" But obviously we have stuff in common. And we're having a good time.

But. I'm in a cocoon with Jewel. Plus Simon and I barely know each other. Maybe this is all about my new longer legs. Is that possible?

We look at the water. He stands up and says, "Parent time. Gotta go."

I nod, not sure if I should stand up and walk with him. Then he takes off. "See ya."

I keep staring at the water, sitting on the bench. *See ya.* The most enigmatic phrase ever. See me when? See me intentionally? I hope so. Soon.

Twenty minutes of agonizing later, I float to the bus stop.

.

.

.

Chapter Five

Of course I can't sleep. I talk to my Dove Girl. "It felt like a movie. Like I was just watching some other girl." But I don't need anyone to tell me that it really happened. I know just from the way my lips, still, feel different.

"I'm tingling."

Time passes.

I hate that I can't talk to Jewel. It's the first time I've kept anything from him. Still. I can't.

Sleepless, I turn toward the wall. I fold my hands together under my pillow, so that they're holding each other. Maybe this pose will help me sleep. Maybe this curl to my legs.

I sit up and look at my Dove Girl in the half-light. She's just a few black lines on a beige background.

I catch sight of myself in the silver frame, barely lit by the streetlight coming through my window. Half of one blue eye, a sliver of nose. No dove.

"Dove Girl," I whisper. "Let me get to dreaming."

I lie down, turn over again, and look out the window by my window seat. Even in the dark night, the tree outside looks so full that I feel like I'm in the jungle, not the city. It's hard to believe that the biggest SUV I've ever seen is parked by the curb waiting for my neighbor, the health-food mogul, to drive it downtown. That we're not all running

around in loincloths, befriending monkeys and eating co-
conuts for dinner. That we're not watched by lions.

I can't stay in bed. I put my feet on the floor and appre-
ciate the hardwood under my bare toes. I tiptoe across my
small room to the door, down the stairs, to the front door.
It's unlocked. My parents are way too trusting.

The October rain is cold, but painless. It feels refreshing, better than sunshine. I want to take off my T-shirt and
be naked, but that's just for a second. I have neighbors. I'm
no jungle princess.

I put my face to the sky and stand next to the tree that
reaches up to my window. Its trunk is so wide. I can't imagine how old this tree is. Jewel and I used to sneak out here
when we were in middle school. One late night, I asked
him what he thought it felt like to be a fish, to breathe
underwater. He said if you were a fish you wouldn't even
think about it.

That idea's followed me since: You do what comes natu-
rally to you without even thinking about it.

I tell myself that, as I struggle to get Dove Girl–esque
peace about myself. If you were a fish, you could breathe
underwater.

You're Alice. Find your peace. Go back to bed.

In the morning I go downstairs to find that Dad has
been on his Sunday walk to Caffe Ladro. He's brought me
back a vanilla latte and a cranberry muffin.

"I was just thinking of waking you before this coffee
turns into lukewarm flavored milk," he says.

"That would imply that I was asleep. Which is sort of true, but sort of not."

He offers to pick up some valerian root at the health-food place later, to help me sleep.

We settle in at the table, Dad reading the paper.

"Where's Mom?"

"Knitting class. She's learning how to do a beanie today."

I nod. My mom tried to teach me how to knit a scarf, but it turned out all clumpy. She swears it was just weird yarn, but I am completely unskilled in the art of tying knots with needles.

The phone rings and Dad answers.

"Oh, hi there!" He looks at me. It must be Jewel. Dad hands me the phone and goes back to reading about our dangerously hot planet.

"I'm psyched about looking for my Bath costume," Jewel says. "The bloodier the better. Maybe I can be a zombie type of thing? A corpse, risen from the grave? Leaving a trail of decomposition in my wake."

I won't mention Simon. Because, really, no one wants a mess. But it will show on my face. This thing that happened yesterday.

In the junk shop Jewel and I look at old hats, old board games, old valentines, old shoes, many old dresses.

I find a powder blue tux on the rack at the back of the store.

"You need this." I finger the white ruffles on the shirt.

I can tell by his smirk that he loves it.

"You can be a lounge singer for the Bath. A dead lounge singer. I'll do your makeup with our old Goth stuff."

In eighth grade, we had a short flirtation with the powers of darkness. Strictly as a fashion statement.

"Yes!" He's grinning like crazy. "And let's find one of those things, those hatchet-through-the-heads? Ya know?"

"Perfecto," I say. "I'll look around while you try that on. It better fit."

"It totally better," he says as he goes to the dressing room.

I look around until Jewel calls me over. The pants are a little big, but we decide he can wear a belt. And the effect makes him look even skinnier than he is, sort of skeleton-like, which is what we want.

Jewel buys the tux for twenty-eight bucks, and I begin to see us at the Bath, me in my dress and Jewel looking hilariously great. We'll dance, silly dances of course. It'll be awesome.

Simon. He'll be there, for sure. "*See ya.*" What is that about? Will he talk to me at the Bath? Before then? At school?

The dance is next Saturday. I'll find out.

Jewel and I go to the counter and the girl remembers us. "Your hem's all done," she says. "Try it on?"

She pulls my dress out of a plastic bag under the counter and I go to the dressing room.

If I borrow heels from my mom, the dress will still

almost touch the floor. Guess my legs aren't getting as long as I thought. That's okay; it'll look like I'm floating. Exactly what I want.

I do a few pseudosexy moves at the mirror, trying out some other personality. I even pull the strap down off my shoulder, baring my skin. Smooth.

Jewel taps on the dressing room door.

I step out, beaming.

He grins back. "You look . . ." Pause. "You look amazing."

He stares at me. Sees me. It feels . . . too real.

"You're too kind," I say, batting my eyelashes. "But your words have saved you from my lizard-gut potions."

I do a scary-witch cackle as I close the dressing room door. I can still feel his eyes on me.

Bags in hand, we go out to the sidewalk. "Gotta return this," Jewel says as he pulls a Japanimation DVD out of his camera bag.

So we walk over to Rain City, the video store. When we get there, I wait by the life-sized cardboard cutout of Hannibal Lecter that permanently stands guard over the checkout counter. Jewel goes to find our video store friend, Tommy.

They emerge from behind the Directors to Watch section. "Greetings, darlings." Tommy gives me a one-armed hug.

Jewel pulls the tux out of his plastic bag and I pull out my dress.

"Fabulous," says Tommy.

We grin. Jewel puts his suit on the counter, grabs the dress from me, and waltzes with it. He dances with exaggerated steps. He hums, does a dip.

"You're actually going to the Bath?" Tommy asks. "I thought it was cheese."

We nod. Jewel turns in small circles.

"Tommy," I say. "The Bath is a thing to talk about over your cafeteria fish sticks. There will be cheerleaders in attendance."

Maybe I shouldn't make fun of cheerleaders so much now that I'm . . . whatever. Now that I'm doing whatever I'm doing with Simon.

"Yeah," says Jewel. "I wouldn't be surprised if they wear their uniforms as costumes. Carry around their pom-poms."

"In my day," Tommy says, which means three years ago, when he was a student at our high school, "the Bath was like twenty of us who didn't want to go around toilet-papering the neighborhood."

"Yeah, but with that whole curfew thing last year," Jewel says, " 'cause of those guys who broke some police cruiser's windows, people are into the idea of drinking punch labeled 'Bat's Blood.' "

"The powers that be actually had us sign pledges in homeroom," I tell Tommy. "Saying that we agree to behave if they don't turn us into pumpkins at eight p.m. It's really gonna bring out the spike-the-punch crowd. They have nothing else to do."

A woman comes up to Tommy, asking him if something with a cartoon devil on its cover is appropriate for her four-year-old son. Her boy holds on to her legs from behind, peeking out us like we're cannibals, or some other scary thing.

Tommy gives me a kiss on the cheek, and one to Jewel.

Back on the sidewalk, Jewel says, "Troll?" We haven't been to visit the troll statue in a while, even though it's right here in Fremont. I always forget how gigantic it is—and then I'm amazed. Maybe the troll is where I'll tell Jewel about Simon. The kiss. Or maybe I'll never tell him. Maybe it'll never happen again and I won't have to worry about it.

"Troll," I say, and we begin to walk uphill. When we get up to Thirty-sixth, I stop and look back at the main stretch of Fremont. The bridge is going up. Three tall sailboats float in a line, waiting to go through.

Jewel stands beside me, breathing. If I moved my arm two inches, we'd be touching. Part of me really wants to touch his skin. It's like there's a zap of energy between our bodies, and our touching would either create a spark or be like an unplugging.

Jewel nods toward the bridge. "I love having drawbridges in town. It reminds me of some other time."

"When people weren't in such a hurry."

"I wonder what he does up in the tower. The controller guy."

We start walking again.

"I guess I'd sketch," Jewel says. "You'd probably sleep."

I don't sleep well at night because I think.

Thinking is the number one enemy of dreaming.

Dreams are what I need.

In dreams, I know everything, and nothing makes sense in that perfect way that's sort of Zen. Like, the sky is totally not supposed to be that color. But cool. Let's go fly a kite anyway. We're feeling okay.

It's always we. I think in terms of we.

Me and Jewel. Me and Simon, maybe. Me and me.

I exhale. "If I could sleep up there, I'd definitely do it."

We walk another block and are at the giant stone troll. It sits, menacing, under the 99 freeway. The troll's left hand crushes a real VW Beetle; that car used to travel the streets, but now it's in a constant state of about-to-be-eaten.

We barely hear the traffic above our heads as we climb the rocks to the troll's back.

Jewel is just ahead of me. I stumble and he turns around to grab my hand. We each have our junk shop bag in one hand, and now we have each other's fingers in the other.

We reach the troll's shoulders, up where we can lean back against his head. Jewel keeps my hand. We let our bags rest on the stone.

Then my planet wobbles.

His hand.

That wanting-to-be-close feeling starts to come over me again. I have the urge to lay my head on Jewel's sweatshirt, on his shoulder. To feel how solid he is.

Did kissing Simon release something in me? Or would I feel this way toward Jewel right now anyway?

As if we're at the slow-motion point in a movie, Jewel reaches across my body to my cheek. He pulls my face toward his. His fingers feel like hot ice. They're cold but they burn me.

My eyes close as he kisses me.

I kiss him back, a dream I've never had.

This kiss is so soft, it's almost like rain falling on my face.

I've never realized the softness of Jewel's hair before. His skin.

Jewel kissing me, me kissing him, feels like a rocket. Like blastoff.

Finally, I pull away.

I'm thinking we shouldn't be doing this. I'm thinking it feels too real. I'm thinking. Simon.

Jewel's eyes are talking. They sparkle, and say yes, and please.

It's the please that gets me. The glint of the question, of please kiss me again and please mean it and please let's be together.

Because with Jewel and me, anything more than this, more than one kiss, means we're a couple.

I'm thinking.

He says, "Wow."

I think, Tell me about it.

I think, Have you honed your mind-reading skills yet, 'cause I hope not.

He leans toward me.

He lets out his breath.

His lips are like the rain.

Ten, nine, eight.

The pressure in me builds.

Seven.

I push him away.

He closes his eyes. Leans against the stone of the troll.

He leans forward. He tells me everything with those eyes. He tells me I'm all he wants. He tells me I'm perfect.

I say, "I better get home for dinner."

He knows we don't eat till seven.

He shuts his eyes. Climbs down the troll's hill.

He pauses by the troll's gigantic thumb. He doesn't look at me again. He jumps to the sidewalk.

I watch him go.

My heart just beats and beats and beats and Jewel and I and—

We really kissed. This heartbeat might be a happy roller-coaster rush if it had happened one week ago. But now. It's a two-guys-at-once-two-kisses-you-have-to-choose.

And I don't know if my heart can survive that kind of beating.

Chapter Six

.

.

.

In sixth grade, I tell my Dove Girl, Jewel and I would sneak out of our houses at night and lie under the tree in my front yard. We'd pretend to be on another planet. All we could see were shadowed leaves and night-cloudy sky through the branches. Sometimes it rained on us. We wore our pajamas there; sometimes all I wore was a big T-shirt. We talked about things like life on Mars. We whispered.

Under the tree in the drizzle, we had our first kiss. My first kiss. His first kiss. Our first kiss.

But I don't actually count it as a real kiss. It was more of a peck. It didn't change anything between us.

Not like today at the troll.

When he kissed me for the second time ever today, it felt amazing.

His lips, like the soft rain.

But I pushed him away.

I just don't know. I don't know if I should kiss Jewel.

It's like we've always been one step away from Couple-hood and kissing him is like a promise to him, that I'm saying we'll be in Couplehood for sure and forever.

And, okay, yeah, to me a kiss means a lot too.

I'm still thinking about it, aren't I? But should I be? Do I want to move to Couplehood with Jewel? Further into our cocoon? Or do I want to leave the cocoon? Does my answer change when I think about Simon Murphy?

One thing's for sure. My Dove Girl has sent me way more than I asked for.

At lunch on Monday, I sit alone. Jewel has lunch fifth period and I have it sixth. Clara and Jeremy don't show.

When Simon puts his tray down across from me, I sit up a little bit on my plastic stool. *"See ya"* meant "I'll sit with you at lunch in front of the whole world!"

Out of the corner of my eye, I see Simon's crew at their usual table: Mike Corrigan and another guy arm wrestling, a girl shredding an orange with her manicured nails.

I'm looking at Simon and his dimple. Right by his lips.

I want to touch his skin. Just like I wanted to touch Jewel's yesterday.

"Glorious meal, eh?" He waves his hand like a game show hostess across his yellow plastic tray.

I say, "Gee. You're easy to please."

"Not when it comes to girls."

Whoa.

Two tables away, his friends huddle around Corrigan. Yesterday he found out he'd won a football scholarship to the University of Washington. Everyone's drooling over him.

I point my chin toward them and say, "My dad worked at Udub."

"Good school."

"So, Mike's gonna be on scholarship?"

I want to know why Simon isn't over there celebrating.

He's eating carrot sticks. Simon Murphy is sitting across from me eating carrot sticks. Which he brought from home. Like we're sitting in his kitchen.

Our first public appearance.

I'm so, so glad that Jewel isn't here to see.

"Well, listen," Simon says. "I wanted to talk to you about something."

"Something, eh? Sounds thrilling."

"Bloodbath." He smiles. Chomps a carrot stick. "Are you going?"

This is so not just *"See ya."*

"I'm gonna be a witch."

"Well," he says, "how are you getting there?"

"Broomstick, duh."

"That's only for hags," he says. "I'll drive you."

Simon Murphy is asking me to the Bloodbath. Simon Murphy, who dated a senior cheerleader. Simon Murphy, who knows about octopi. Simon Murphy.

But I'm going with Jewel!

That's just for goofs, though. That's not *this*. That's not a date. That's just a thing. Like any other thing with Jewel. But, God, he just kissed me. So it would be a date. Wouldn't it?

I have to say something now, though. To Simon. Jewel can deal. Right? Because I want to go with Simon. I do. Yes.

"Oh. Well. Okay then."

How can I do this? What about Jewel? This isn't me.

I could still back out.

"I'll pick you up."

I stare at my tray. I'm going to the dance with Simon

Murphy. Instead of going with my blend-into-the-lockers best friend. Who kissed me yesterday. Who I kissed back.

Jewel and I picked out our costumes together. I'm supposed to do his makeup. We told Tommy. He kissed me! I let him! How can I go with Simon?

How can I not?

Simon collects his things. "Catch you later."

All through English class, I alternate between popping my leg up and down in excitement over Simon and freezing in contemplation of Jewel.

We're having an assembly, so no Spanish today. Thankfully, I won't have to deal with being in the same room with both of them. But Jewel's in my study hall.

I shut my eyes. I think of Edgar Allan Poe, "The Tell-Tale Heart," the story where that guy murders another guy and almost gets away with it but turns super-guilty and has a breakdown because he's sure people can hear the corpse's heart beating underneath the floorboards, where he has put the body. My heart is like that.

I'm afraid that somehow Jewel can sense what's going on. And I'm afraid that Simon will realize how much this means to me. Which is how much exactly? On a scale of one to ten. And why? I have a date to the big dance. So? Now will my life be complete? Will I be, like, Halloween Queen? I so need to get a grip.

Dove Girl, quiet my heart.

After English, in my locker, I find a note from Jewel.

I look at it, notebook paper written on in blue felt-tip. Folded up, *Alice* written in tiny letters on the front.

My heart beats.

He's included a photo of the troll. Black-and-white. Beautiful.

Alice, the note says. *I'm writing because I'm afraid if I try to talk to you, I'll just freeze up. I guess I've wanted to kiss you for a while, but I didn't mean for it to actually happen. Or did you like it? Do you want to go to the dance with me, as my date? I'll buy you a corsage made for a witch. Wilted to perfection.*

For one whole second, I'm excited. Then I remember.

I'm so not showing up to study hall. If Jewel's heard about Simon by now, which is possible, I can't face him. If he hasn't, I still can't face him, because I need to tell him that I won't be his date and that I'm ditching him for the Bloodbath entirely.

When did I turn into this person?

I feel horrible. I'm *ditching* Jewel. I'm basically forcing him to hate me. But I'm also allowed to have a crush, right? I never promised Jewel anything. He's my best friend. Not my boyfriend.

Thank God Mr. Smith is the study hall monitor. I wait outside the room until I see him making his way down the hall.

"Mr. Smith," I say when he gets there. "Could I spend this period in the studio? I really want to do some water-colors."

He writes me a pass.

Just by avoiding Jewel right now, I feel like I'm breaking the rules.

I get out my notebook, tear off a piece of paper, and write a note.

I ask him to meet me at the troll after school.

I walk down the empty hall, fast so I won't flip out, and I slip the note into his locker.

The VW's rear windshield is newly decorated with a Day-Glo heart, spray-paint pink, filled in with squiggles. A garnish of love graffiti for the beast's meal.

I lean against the troll's fist, out of the misty rain, waiting for Jewel. I think about what to say to him. *I love you as a friend.* . . . *It's not you, it's me.* . . .

Jewel walks from the direction of school, his hood up against the drizzle and his eyes down.

He gets to where I am. He doesn't talk. He doesn't look at me.

"I got your note."

"I figured." He moves his gaze to the pink heart.

"I don't know what to say." I close my eyes, then open them and speak to his forehead. "I can't go with you. I have . . . a date, sort of."

I let my gaze meet his. My eyes instantly water. "But I still want to hang out with you. You're . . . my best friend."

He finally looks at me. He's heard. It's obvious. His eyes are empty. Someone slapped Simon five on a new chick or something, in front of Jewel. Possibly on purpose.

In this instant, I want to erase everything with Simon

and just go back to normal with Jewel. But I also know that it's impossible. Because now Jewel and I have our own kiss-weirdness so even if there weren't a Simon Murphy in my life, there would not be normal with Jewel, either.

"Why don't you come for dinner," I say. "Lasagna. Saturday before the dance."

He looks back at the VW. "Wouldn't your boyfriend be pissed?"

He turns, keeps his head down as he walks through the rain.

I don't think about it; I just run after him. "Hey," I say. "Hey."

He turns around.

"That's not fair. For you to be mad at me for having a date to the Bath."

He just looks at me, rain falling between us.

I go on. "I know we were supposed to go together. We do everything together. But you know . . . I'm allowed to have a date who's not you. Isn't that okay? And you might . . . go out with someone."

Jewel and someone else? The thought is like someone stealing from me.

He stands there.

"Is it because Simon's . . . what? Popular?"

"Alice, that's so not it." He walks away again. I don't follow him.

I walk home feeling like something so low. Like I deserve to be eaten by the troll.

Because what Jewel really meant was: I'm breaking his heart.

.

.

.

Chapter Seven

When I go to bed and close my eyes, I hear Jewel's voice, shaking. So I sit up and trace my Dove Girl with the tip of my finger, starting with her eyes, extending to her long nose, her uneven heart of a mouth. Then her head; lastly, the place where her skin turns into the wings of a dove. I try to memorize this shape. Peace. What it is to be still, calm.

I've tried drawing her in my sketchbook. She ends up too pointy or too mean-looking. Mean like me, according to Jewel. Maybe. Probably.

What if it were two weeks ago? What if Jewel had kissed me then and Simon and I had never hung out? And kissed? Then would I go with Jewel to the Bath as his date? Would I become his girlfriend?

What ifs. That's all I've got because my Dove Girl doesn't talk back. She just sits there, looking like the Buddha or something.

The Buddha reminds me of Vanessa's new Zen thing.

I wonder what Vanessa would say about my boy situation. As if I would ever ask her.

I already know the answer, anyway. Deep down. Yeah. Yes. If Jewel had kissed me and Simon hadn't, I'd be with Jewel. I'd be his.

We'd stay in our cocoon.

∾

Tuesday morning, I take a quick shower, put on my sweater, jeans, and orange puffy vest, grab an apple in the kitchen, yell goodbye to my parents shuffling around in their room, and start my walk.

Dad used to drive me to school on his way to the university. But I like walking. School is one mile away, almost exactly, which gives me enough time to mellow before hitting the hallowed halls.

I head down Phinney and almost step on a slug. I think it's a fat stick at first. Then I stoop to look at it. It's a teeny alien, with those eyes on top of its head. Now that I think of it, *I* feel a little alien: a strange girl on an even stranger planet that should look familiar but doesn't.

I remember the Chihuly slug from the museum. I have glassblowing on Saturday.

I keep walking, careful where I step.

Jewel and I usually meet at Thirty-fourth and Phinney. He's not here.

Still mad, then. Still . . . whatever. Hurt.

I keep walking, having an imaginary conversation with him.

"Morning," I say, in my head.

"Morning," he says. "How's my girl?"

And his eyes shift toward me.

I smile.

And then maybe he'd touch my elbow and we'd walk along. He'd tell me his dreams.

I reach Ultra Convenience, four blocks from school,

and Simon's car is parked out front. I stop, considering running into him.

He walks out of the store.

"Hey."

"Hey."

"I'll drive you the rest of the way."

Nothing wrong with this.

I ignore the swarm of bees in my stomach as I get into his car.

He gives me some Juicy Fruit from his fresh pack. You can totally smell that stuff on his breath all day. Now it'll be on mine, too.

We drive slowly past the park.

"I wish I could still play at the park," I say.

"Like a kid?"

Maybe I'm being weird, talking about this stuff. Maybe he wants to talk about parties or something.

Before I know it, we're in the school parking lot. Then he's holding open the front door for me.

I don't think anyone even saw us come in together. Good. Or maybe not.

Mr. Smith asked me to come up with a design for the cover of our "portfolio showcase," which will come out right before Thanksgiving break. I'm doodling.

For the showcase, Mr. Smith takes photos of our paintings, drawings, and sculptures and then gets the portfolio made at Kinko's. If we have a few bake sales, we can get color copies.

I guess it's an honor to be asked to do the cover, but really I think Mr. Smith suggested it because lately I've been doing more staring at the wall than actual art.

I doodle the shape of an artist's palette, but that's lame.

Apparently, Vanessa thinks so too. "Creative much?" She peeks over my shoulder.

"Constantly."

She raises the red oil-soaked brush in her hand over my paper and for a second I think she's going to ruin my scribbles.

She lets the brush dangle only millimeters away from my paper.

"Va—" I start, but before I can finish she's walking toward the sink.

That night after dinner, Mom and Dad ask me to walk to the café by the railroad tracks to see Jewel's photos on the wall.

"All right," I say.

"Think he'll want to come with us?" Mom asks.

There's no way I can invite him anywhere right now. "He's in the darkroom."

At the café, I sip ice water while my parents drink decaf Americanos as they walk around to each of Jewel's photos. I stay close. I spend as much time looking at my feet as I do looking at the photos.

"Grayfur is so cute," my mom says.

Hearing the cat's name makes me flash on such a vivid memory of tying on her superhero cape; I feel stricken. "Yeah."

Mom puts her arm around me. "Sick of these photos?" she asks. She thinks I'm bored. My own mother can't even tell when I'm sad.

"Not at all," I say.

Part of me wishes that Jewel would come in right now and we'd just face each other. It has to happen sooner or later. If I haven't lost my best friend forever.

Chapter Eight

.

.

.

It's like Jewel and I had agreed to avoid each other.

He misses two days of study hall.

I plan to skip the school art show on Thursday night. My entry is one of the watercolors of the canal that got rejected by the Green Bean. It could be hanging with Jewel's photos there right now, but it's not good enough. So it's tacked to a bulletin board in the school lobby. I wish I had a beautiful glass sculpture to display—something colorful and amazing.

Mr. Smith expects us all to go, but I hope he won't notice if I'm not there. In a pinch, I could mention what's going on. Not that I'd tell him everything, but he'd probably understand that if Jewel and I are fighting, it would be officially not cool for us both to go to the show.

The people from my workshop set up for the show during class on Thursday. I mix up fruit punch while Vanessa cuts a block of sharp cheddar into little cubes and sticks toothpicks in the middle. The toothpicks have those sparkly cellophane curlicues at their tops, some kind of fancy.

I remember a time in fifth grade when she was at my house and we made cookies with whatever we could yank out of my cupboard: marshmallows, hot cocoa mix, butterscotch chips, walnuts.

We leave everything on Mr. Smith's desk so he can put it in the staff room fridge.

"Hey, Vanessa," I say. "What are you putting in the show?"

She looks at me from under her heavy black eyelashes. "That city I made."

The city is cardboard boxes painted in metallics. She made them somehow look heavy and solid. Jewel mentioned wanting to photograph the city. It's good. Unique. "Cool."

"You?"

"Nothing special."

We're standing here in the art room, talking. Why do I feel so uneasy?

I pick up my bag and get out of the room. Vanessa's schoolbag is made out of silver duct tape. She follows me.

"Did you make that bag?" I ask her.

"Yeah," she says. "It's easy."

It reminds me of doing magazine collages with her on my bedroom floor; we ran out of glue and resorted to masking tape. The results weren't pretty. I smirk at the memory.

"What?"

"I was just . . . do you remember those collages we did?"

She stops walking and looks at me.

"Collages? For Smith's class?"

I guess she doesn't remember. I guess it doesn't matter. "Never mind."

We keep walking and, at the door, go our separate ways.

~

I can't stay away from the art show completely. I do care about it. Any event that brings out the curlicue tooth-picks is something I don't want to miss, pathetic as that sounds. I don't get into the coffee shop art shows like Jewel does; I've gotta take what I can get.

Thursday night, I'm staked out on the brick side of the school, kneeling in the garden by the big window. I've worn a black sweatshirt, hoping I won't be spotted.

Inside, Mr. Smith is gesturing at Vanessa as everyone mills around, eating the cheese and drinking the punch. Clara and Jeremy hold hands.

No one is standing in front of my painting. I kind of want to bite the bullet and go in.

I watch Jewel in front of his exhibit, up-close photos of the troll. Like the one with my note. They show the troll's fingers, his one eye, the VW. The grooved details of his wavy hair. The pink graffiti.

Vanessa walks up to Jewel, smiling.

They talk.

He touches her upper arm, bare because she's wearing a black sequined tank top. Just once. But it's enough to make my stomach jump.

I'm pretty enough; Vanessa's maybe prettier. I'm an okay artist; she's great. I'm out here in the shadows.

We have a lot of classes together, which is just the way it works. The person you want to forget about, the gods of scheduling make sure you spend your high school years constantly seated behind.

Our friendship was just a kid thing. I guess what we are now is more . . . competitive, if anything. She probably doesn't think about me. Except maybe in one way.

I've always had one thing that she wants like crazy. Jewel. The most creative guy at school. The artist. And I had the ability to inspire him. His only friend.

Until now.

Friday, in art workshop, I stand at an easel by the window, looking out toward the empty courtyard. I busy myself with the painting I've already started as a Christmas gift for my parents. It's a portrait of them, but I'm trying to do it all in little dots, spots of watercolor that add up to being people. I spend most of the class trying to swirl a good blue for my dad's eyes.

Vanessa is quiet today.

When Mr. Smith announces that it's time to clean up, I see what she's been working on. She's cut up a bunch of soda cans. The tops, with their tabs, litter her table. She's fashioned a crown and a scepter.

It's a scary thought, a world where I turn my back and Vanessa becomes royalty.

.

.

.

Chapter Nine

I wake up and think, *Dove Girl, tonight's the night.* Blood-bath night. Halloween.

Part of me feels like my witch dress is appropriate because I'm being a witch to Jewel.

The other part of me is totally excited. Showing up with Simon will be a major thing. People are about to see me differently. The new Alice. Interesting. Tonight I will turn heads. Vanessa won't outshine me. No girl will.

I'm grateful that my glassblowing class is today; otherwise, I don't know how I'd pass a whole Saturday before the dance without exploding.

The front of the studio is a store, selling beautiful, swirly-colored lamps and bowls. I check out a green bowl and can't help imagining Jewel's hazel eyes.

No. Today is not about Jewel, or missing him, or how I might've screwed up our friendship.

I finish browsing and head to the back of the shop.

The only person there is a guy in a tie-dyed T-shirt, with a long ponytail. His back is to me. Must be Jim.

I'm nervous. Where are the other students? What am I doing here?

He turns around and smiles at me.

"Welcome," he says. "You are?"

"Alice Davis."

"Welcome, Alice Davis. Happy Halloween. I'm Jim." He's very much a hippie; he seems blissed out. ·

I hear footsteps and turn to see a middle-aged woman walking in, wearing hiking pants and a white tank top.

Right behind her is Mandy Walker. From the elite who sit at Simon's lunch table. Just what I didn't want.

"Hey," she says. "Alice, right? I'm so glad I recognize someone here!"

She's here, so she can't be all bad.

"Yeah. Alice. Hey."

Jim asks us all to sit down. Folding chairs wait underneath a shelf full of tools.

Only three people signed up for this class? I guess we'll each be getting a lot of attention.

Never stop spinning. The liquid glass glows orange like the sun, with green and yellow swirls, as I control it at the tip of the blowpipe. It turns in the furnace. I'm spinning hand over hand over hand. This is my best try yet, after three hours of instruction. Jim yells, "Feel the weight of your piece!" "Keep turning!" "To the bench!"

So I go to the bench, turning, quick before the glass hardens. Sit on the bench, spin the blowpipe on the chair's rail, spin, spin. Shape. "Chill the bottom half with air!" Jim shouts. I keep spinning with one hand and grab the air hose with the other. It feels awkward, but I manage to let air out of the hose and keep spinning the glass.

The glass is cooling.

Back to the furnace. Make the glass orange again.

The heat smells like burnt marshmallows.

"To the bench!"

Heat it up. Then cool it. Use air. Use water. Heat it up. Everything has to be perfect or my piece will be destroyed.

But that's okay. I am in control of this.

Sweaty and flushed, but happy, I say thank you to Jim and walk out to the store. Mandy is admiring a pink lamp. "How long do you think till we're this good?"

I think of Dale Chihuly. "Years and years." Neither one of our first attempts at a bowl survived. Jim says that's normal. He's a cool guy—went from blissed out to kind of militant the moment we got our hands on the tools, but that makes sense. I was a little terrified of getting burnt or burning someone else.

"Are you doing the follow-up class?" she asks.

It's only twenty bucks to come back in for a private or pairs session with Jim. "I think so. I really liked it."

"Me too."

Talking to her, with her standing there just as sweaty as me, I almost forget who Mandy is at school, one of the kids Jewel and I always thought seemed silly, kind of stupid. She's not like that.

We walk out together. "Raining again," she says.

"As always."

We pass the scone shop and I'm dying for a latte. She says, "Want to go in?"

"My need for caffeine shows?"

She grins and opens the door.

Chunky Glasses isn't here; the weekend girl is a pink-haired baby-doll-dress-wearing punk girl. Her nose stud looks a lot like Vanessa's. She gets our lattes and Mandy and I sit at a table.

"So," Mandy says, "I have gymnastics in an hour. Can't stay long."

"Cool." I wonder what it's like to be able to use your body that way. "That must help with cheerleading."

"Oh, yeah. Been doing it my whole life, practically."

"Like me and art."

"But this was your first time glassblowing?"

"Yeah. I usually paint. Well. I try to paint. What about you? I've never seen you around the art studio at school."

"The art studio?" Mandy looks straight at me. "I wouldn't fit in. The art crowd is . . . kind of intimidating. Like there's a weirdness factor that I don't have?"

Mandy Walker, cheerleader, is intimidated by *us*?

"Well . . . ," I say. "Some people are like that, I guess." We sip.

"So I heard you're Simon's date to the Bath?"

I almost choke. "Yep."

"He's such a nice guy."

"Who are you going with?"

"Solo." Wow. I have a date and Mandy doesn't? "I'll just dance with whoever."

If I went by myself, I'd stand as close to the wall as possible.

"Cool. What are you dressing as?"

"Butterfly." I think back to my conversation with Jewel about the Beautiful People using the dance as an excuse to wear leotards in public.

"Cool."

We finish our lattes and head out. It's not until I'm almost home that I realize she didn't make a big deal at all about me and Simon. Maybe he was never as far out of reach as I thought he was.

After I shower off the studio grime, I eat lasagna with my parents. "I really liked it," I say. "Definitely going again."

It's hard to let them know how bubbly excited I am about the whole day. Simon. The Bath. A new art medium. A possible new friend. A possible whole new future. I just say, "It was great."

Mom sits on the edge of the dry bathtub as I attempt to slide my feet into her two-inch black special-occasion heels.

She used to work at Nordstrom, so she knows a lot about fashion and beauty.

Seeing her sitting there reminds me of the time I had a horrible flu in third grade. She drew me bath after bath because it was the only thing that would keep me from feeling my fever. I'd wait for the tub to fill, sitting naked in a towel against the sink cabinet, sucking on purple Popsicles.

Now she's wearing an all-white sweat suit and fairy wings.

The shoes are on. "Okay, eye shadow," I say. "Make me look . . . smoky."

Mom stands up and when I close my eyes to let her transform me, she says, "You're beautiful. Your date is one lucky boy."

I blush.

"How come we've never met him before?" She finishes my makeup and I open my eyes.

"Because I didn't know him before."

"Well, your dad and I will meet him tonight." She untwists the cap of my lipstick: Cherry Pop, the closest thing I own to blood.

"Yeah," I say. "That actually makes me think of something."

"Hmm?" She hands me the lipstick tube and a square of toilet paper for blotting.

"Don't mention Jewel tonight, okay? When Simon is here." I put on the lipstick and blot. "They're not really friends."

"What's going on between you and Jewel lately?"

I wish I knew. "We kind of had a fight." I throw away the toilet paper.

"About . . ."

"I think I was feeling kind of stuck, just having one friend."

"That's understandable."

"I guess."

"But just because you want to have more friends, that doesn't mean you can't still be close with Jewel."

"That's the thing. My new person to hang out with is someone Jewel would never be friends with."

"That sounds pretty closed-minded. Not like Jewel."

"Mom, it's high school. There's popularity stuff."

"Well, I miss Jewel."

"Me too." My eyes immediately start to tear and I have to take a deep breath. I really do miss him.

Tonight is about me and Simon, though. And that's exciting.

She hands me the shiny satin witch hat she made for me, and we pin it on.

The doorbell rings and I hear my dad stomping to the door, being Frankenstein as he does every Halloween. Trick-or-treaters scream out their line.

My mom leaves the bathroom to join him, hugging me quickly and then plucking her fairy wand from the sink.

No more missing Jewel. Tonight is about a Dove Girl wish come true.

In my witchy mind, I am kissed.

The doorbell rings again and I catch myself holding my breath. Is it kids or—?

"You must be Simon," Mom says. I breathe, stand up, smooth my dress, adjust my hat, check the mirror one last time, and head downstairs.

Simon's wearing his football uniform. He hands me a ghost-shaped box of candy. "Like my costume?"

I glance at Mom. Is she thinking I'm crazy for going to the dance with some football player instead of Jewel? "Is that a costume?"

"I'm Mike Corrigan." Simon turns around. "Number twelve, see."

"Oh," I say, my eyes lingering south of his number twelve. Then remembering Mom. "Yeah. Thanks for the candy!"

My dad comes out of the kitchen with a huge bowl of peanut butter cups.

I take a step and clutch the banister. Whoa. Careful not to fall right out of Mom's heels. They're already starting to hurt, too.

I hand her the ghost candies. I'm sure she thinks it's the cutest gesture ever. Score one for Simon Murphy, he of the unimaginative costume who brings thoughtful gifts.

"Mom, Dad, this is Simon Murphy."

"Trick or treat." Simon grins and his little half-moon dimple almost does me in.

Dad hands Simon a peanut butter cup.

I assure my parents that my cell phone is with me, and then Simon and I are out the door. I'm still walking awkwardly in the heels, but that's more witchlike, anyway. Crotchety. But, God. I wanted to be pretty tonight. Still do. And how will I dance if I can't even walk to the car? "Hold on, I gotta go switch shoes."

I replace the heels with my Pumas and take off again, passing my parents in the kitchen. They stand at the counter, arms around each other, chomping chocolate, and smile at me.

Simon leans into me as we walk across my yard. "You're hot, even if you are a witch."

This dance is going to be perfect.

∽

At school, we park on a side street. I'm careful of puddles as we come together at the front of his car. It's not raining, thankfully, but the sidewalk is its usual wet self.

"Let's make a quick stop first," he says.

"Okay."

I follow Simon to the park. I can feel how damp the grass is even through my sneakers. It's refreshing. Something about this is so quintessentially fall. Running through the wet grass on a semi-chilly October night, all dressed up.

He sits on a swing even though it's wet. "You said you wanted to play."

He remembered.

"Let's swing!" he says.

I step up to the swing next to his and grab the chain. "I can't believe you remembered I thought about coming here."

"I remember everything you've said to me."

Is that a line? Do I care? This is so sweet.

"The swing's wet," I say. "I don't want my dress to get wet." It crosses my mind that he might ask me to sit on his lap. Then he gestures to his lap.

This is so like a movie.

I walk over to him. He reaches for my waist and pulls me down to him.

"This isn't how kids play," I say.

"You're gorgeous."

He digs his feet into the grass below us and we sway. I feel his breath on my neck. I feel gorgeous.

His eyes are closed. His hands are on my hips. This

might be the most rewarding thing ever: wanting a guy and getting him.

Our reverie ends when a truck passes.

"Race ya to the slide," he says.

Simon wins. When I get up the ladder and reach the slide's platform, he's waiting for me, kneeling. I kneel in front of him, careful of my dress.

"I've never kissed a witch," he says. And then he does, over and over.

"I've never kissed Mike Corrigan," I finally tell him.

"And you never will."

"No!" We're laughing.

On our way to the Bath, he holds me like I am a prize, arm all the way around my middle, frequently squeezing. It's like he's making sure I'm real. I squeeze him back.

Jack-o'-lanterns with jagged mouths grimace on the steps of the school.

When we reach the door, Simon holds it open and ushers me in, his free hand between my shoulder blades. People definitely notice us. A devil holding the hand of a genie waves to Simon.

It still smells like chalk in here, but the school feels different tonight. Magical? Okay, that's going too far. But special. The school's all dressed up for Halloween too.

I'm not the only witch in the lobby, but one of the two others just has orange yarn stapled to the inside of her pointy hat, something you'd get at the drugstore. The other witch has green warts all over her face. Not attractive.

I spot Clara and Jeremy walking through the lobby, dressed as salt and pepper shakers.

Corrigan is over by the boys' bathroom, talking to Molly from Spanish class. She's dressed as a purple fairy and he's got Simon's jersey. Her back is turned toward me; her wings shimmer. Corrigan catches my eye. The look in his eyes is . . . I don't know, something like I'm steak and he's really, really hungry.

It's gross. I grab on to Simon's hand.

A guy standing by the water fountain has loads of that fake cobwebby stuff taped around himself and he's got a jump rope sticking out of his white turtleneck.

"Who's the tampon?" asks Simon.

"Eew. I don't know."

Mandy comes out of the bathroom; her butterfly costume isn't slutty like I imagined it might be. She looks really cute in a black minidress with wings and antennae. She waves hello.

Nine Inch Nails is blaring from the gym. I thank my Dove Girl that I have been spared Monster Mash–esque torture.

Again Simon ushers me through the door. It takes my eyes a minute to adjust to the dark.

Smoke fills the corners of the room, from what must be dry ice inside trash cans. The cans have shovels next to them and mounds of dirt, like someone has been digging graves all around the dance floor. Nooses hang from both basketball hoops.

"What's that box by the locker room?" Simon points. It's loud in here.

I can't tell, so I grab his hand and lead him.

I'm pretty sure a football player winks at us.

The box turns out to be a room created from the tall corkboard dividers where our art show was displayed.

Simon pulls me through a black curtain into the box.

We're alone; no teacher. The room is lit by black light. Simon looks like a bright white football ghost with too many teeth.

Stools are scattered around the space with glowing bowls resting on them. I get it. The old Halloween joke, peeled-grape eyeballs and spaghetti brains.

"Hey, Simon, go feel what's in that bowl."

He grabs me by the waist. "I'd rather feel what's in this dress."

Again we kiss like a storm.

It occurs to me that kissing him no longer makes me nervous. It feels natural somehow, like something I just know how to do. I might be growing up after all.

A mermaid and a vampire come through the curtain, he already starting to work on her neck.

I am so not making out in here with other people, even if Simon is breathing into my neck like he never wants to stop.

I grab his hand to lead him back to the dance.

We go toward the entrance, where there are ballots to vote for Halloween Queen and King. We don't vote.

Vanessa is standing by the punch bowl with Nicolai

Gregory. He's dressed as a preppy guy: hair bleached blond, gelled back, argyle sweater, khakis. Boat shoes. All-out fabulous.

She's in a totally eighties hot pink dress. She's wearing a sash that says PROM QUEEN 1980. Black fishnet tights that look like spiderwebs are ripped across her legs. Her face is the color of my watercolor brush cup after I finished my dad's eyes, gray with blue tones. Blood drips at the corners of her eyes. She's a dead prom queen. Her hair is ratted; bed head from the coffin. She holds an empty bottle of Budweiser, like a public service announcement for not drinking and driving.

"Hey, Vanessa Almond looks pretty good," says Simon. "In a scary way."

I nod. I'd be jealous of her costume if I didn't know she's probably drooling about mine too.

Some guys stop to talk to Simon and I wonder what to say to them. Simon hasn't introduced me. Of course, I do have trig with two of them and bio with another one. So we sort of know each other. I'm mulling that over.

Then it happens. Vanessa's king arrives, wearing the soda can crown.

It's Jewel. My Jewel. No, wait. Her Jewel.

He walks over to her, carrying a black rose. He's wearing the powder blue tuxedo. But. He didn't come as a dead lounge singer. He came as Dead Prom King 1980.

He fastens the rose to Vanessa's dress, a corsage.

Jewel pours punch for Vanessa as I stand speechless next to a guy I hardly know.

.

.

.

Chapter Ten

Jewel drinks punch and Vanessa leans in to whisper something to him. He nods. She heads my way, nose in the air like a fashion model.

So this is it. This is the way it is. Jewel with Vanessa. Me with Simon.

"Alice," she says as she reaches Simon and me, "I like your costume."

I just look at her. I want to tell her Jewel's not her friend. He's mine.

Simon jumps in. "We like yours, too."

Vanessa ignores Simon. I've accidentally forced her into a staring contest. She's listening, though. "Thank you so much."

She saunters in the direction of the bathroom. Then she pauses and turns back toward me. She calls out, "Doesn't Julian look great tonight?"

I stifle the urge to run over and scratch her.

"What was that all about?" Simon asks.

"Don't ask me."

"Well, isn't Jewel your best friend, though?"

"Yeah."

"So what's up?"

"With Jewel and Vanessa?"

"With Jewel and you."

"Nothing. You said it. We're friends."

"Definitely not more?"

"No."

"Good," Simon says, " 'cause I wouldn't want my girl-friend to be into another guy."

I'm officially his girlfriend? And he's on record as being jealous. Of Jewel. Not of Corrigan, who looks at me like I'm something to sink his teeth into.

This is what I wanted, I tell myself. Dove Girl, help me keep Simon interested. If I don't, I'll be alone and that will be way worse than where I started.

I take his hand and lead him to the dance floor.

The music is something I don't recognize, fast and without words. Very heavy on the bass.

Simon dances like a jellyfish, loosely wiggling in an ef-fortless way like his limbs had evolved to work in this spe-cific environment.

I hop from one foot to the other, trying to imagine how a witch would get down and boogie. It helps that Simon only takes his hands off me for short stints as he turns in circles.

He does that thing I've seen in music videos, where the guy bends his knees and, like, works his way up the girl's body with his head two inches from her. I try not to look too stiff.

The DJ switches to a slow song, something about moon-light. For the first time, Simon seems awkward. He's bending

his head next to mine, his Nikes only millimeters from my
Pumas, his middle somehow not there.

It takes me a minute to realize that he's all bent on purpose. He's energized. In that particular male way.

Under my makeup, I'm sure my face is as pink as
Vanessa's dress.

I move my hands to Simon's waist. I pull his body
closer to mine. He lets out a sound between a squeak and
a moan.

This is a movie. I am not really doing this.

I'd almost believe that this is not real, because it's so
surreal, me and Simon. Right in the middle of the crowd.
But this feels too good. He bends his head so our fore-
heads touch. I feel like I could fly.

I put my mouth to his neck, leave it there, a twitch
away from kissing.

He puts his hand on the back of my head, works his
fingers through my hair.

The song fades out. Were Vanessa and Jewel watching us?

"Hey, hey," says the DJ, "are you ready to crown one
lucky lady your queen?"

People do little whistles and whoops.

"I said, are you ready?"

Oh, God. School spirit. People roar, so easily excited.
Simon grins at me. He doesn't know how totally turned off
I am by mob mentality.

"That's more like it! Drumroll, please," yells the DJ.
Feet stamp all over the Bath, creating a thunder.

"And the moment has arrived," he continues. "You've voted for your favorite costumes and here they are . . ."

A whispering ripple moves through the crowd.

"Your king, Nicolai Gregory!"

Nicolai walks up to the DJ stand, grinning and waving like the President. It's hilarious.

The DJ continues, "And your queen . . ."

Simon squeezes my hand.

". . . Vanessa Almond!"

Vanessa joins Nicolai. She stands still, her head lolling to one side, her eyes as blank as possible, playing dead.

Their crowns are cardboard covered with foil. Not nearly as cool as the one Vanessa made.

"All right, you two," says the DJ. "Let's see what a royal dance looks like!"

There's no spotlight in the gym, of course, but if there were, this would be the moment when it would shine on Nicolai and Vanessa, as the crowd opens a space for its nobility, then would pan to Jewel across the room as he puts on a smile. He's the date of the queen.

When he's really happy, he doesn't smile. He smirks.

Nicolai and Vanessa sashay around, high drama. If this were the prom, they wouldn't have won. But it's Halloween and they are definitely the strangest pair in school.

The crowd has opened a large circle for them, all eyes on their played-up waltz. The dance only lasts a minute, until Jewel elbows his way through the crowd and enters the circle.

He taps Nicolai on the shoulder, something you'd see

in an old movie. He doesn't, however, ask if he may cut in. He just presses Nicolai out of the way, gently, Nicolai obeying. Then Jewel lays a big kiss on Vanessa.

The crowd, needless to say, goes wild.

Some girl behind me asks her friend, "Who's that cute guy?"

Someone tells her, "I always thought that guy was into guys. He's so *artistic*."

I grab Simon and kiss him.

The girl behind me says, "Wait. Who's she?"

The school might have something to talk about on Monday.

Simon walks me up to my door. "Let's talk," he says, and we sit on the porch swing.

I seriously don't think my brain can handle some big talk right now.

I sit and look at him.

"I just want to say," he says, "that I had a great time tonight."

He's got that dimple out.

"Me too. It was . . . amazing."

"But I'm wondering about why you're quiet."

The dimple is gone. I'm not sure what he's looking for here.

"Am I?" *Definitely not about seeing Jewel with Vanessa,* I think. I sit up and press closer to Simon.

I make a mental note: Be more normal around your boyfriend.

"You should . . . get yourself to bed," he says.

I nod, put my head on his shoulder.

"I'm not your bed," he tells me.

"But you're comfy."

He maneuvers to kiss my forehead. It's so sweet I think I might just crumble right here.

"Night, my little witch." He stands and goes to his car, walking backward down our path, watching me as he goes.

After he drives off, I walk into the dark house, up to my room, and fall asleep in about two seconds. In my dress.

.

.

.

Chapter Eleven

On Sunday, I sit on the couch in my sweatpants and stripy sweater. My dad is outside raking the wet leaves in our front yard. My mom is sitting across from me in the lounger reading a cookbook, armed with index cards and a fountain pen.

I try to read the latest *McSweeney's*. It's a great issue: monster stories. But I'm way too distracted.

The first thing I did this morning was whisper to my Dove Girl. *"Let Simon be worth it,"* I said. *"Let him be worth all this weirdness with Jewel. And whatever is happening with Vanessa."*

I slept well last night, and now it feels like I can't wake up. I drift asleep on the couch, my book open on my stomach, still halfway sitting up, wedged into the armrest.

I wake up to the smell of baking and wander into the kitchen. I touch my hair out of habit. But my ponytail's not there. I never put my hair up after the dance last night, and I think I'll try leaving it down from now on. I look more like Simon's girlfriend this way.

"Oatmeal cookies with butterscotch chips," Mom says, "from a new recipe."

"Yum."

"I thought I'd give us a nice fall treat." She scrapes another cookie onto the plate that already holds a pile. "So, Sleeping Beauty? How was the dance?"

I don't know how to sum it up. I slow-danced. I kissed my date. Simon was wonderful. Jewel . . . was with someone else. "It was basically good."

"Basically?" She scrapes another cookie.

"Just not used to stuff like dances, I guess," I say.

"What about stuff like dates? How'd it go with Simon?"

"It was good."

She must know instinctively, or from my face, that I don't want to say any more. It must've been obvious the moment she met him: Simon should be out of my league. Maybe she's not sure what he's doing with me either.

"I think I made too many cookies," she says, running out of room on her plate. "Why don't you take a Baggie over to Jewel?"

"He's busy."

She hands me a cookie and nods.

I bite.

The cookie tastes so good, sweet yet not too sugary, that I want to eat the whole batch.

I stop myself after three, gulp down some milk, and go to sit on the porch swing.

My *McSweeney's* is on my lap, but all I can think about is: What's with Jewel and Vanessa? Does he really like her? What is going to happen at school?

I need a girlfriend to gush with. I have a boyfriend! He's amazing! We make out!

I wonder if my mom would want to know. Or what she'd want to know. Should I talk to her more?

The problem here is: no precedent. Never before have I fought with Jewel. You can't fight if you're not talking, though, so that makes it even harder to define what's happening between us. Never has there been space between us.

Never before have I had a crush that's turned into something real; never been called someone's girlfriend.

I need to make up the rules for talking about it.

The making out part feels private.

I sit on the porch and daydream, wishing Simon would show up, or call.

Now Dad's working on the Chevy. He's pretty cute out there, wearing a dirty old white T-shirt. I have this image of him putting the training wheels on my first bike, and I swear he was in that same shirt. My dad's one of those guys who never really ages.

"Hey, sweetie," he says as I walk to the car.

"Can I help?"

He looks up, greasy-armed. "Oh, I'm just fiddling."

"Any chance she'll be running for my birthday?"

He grins at me. "We'll see."

My birthday's not until January. I do hope for the car.

"What are you thinking of doing for your sweet sixteen, anyway?" He wipes his hands with a rag.

"Dunno."

"But I assume Jewel will be included?"

Smooth, Dad. "I have no idea."

"What about that Simon? Did you have a good time?"

"He's . . . fun."

"Seemed like a jock."

"Dad, that's such an old-fashioned word."

"So he's not a football player?"

"He's more than that. He's into octopi. He volunteers at the aquarium."

Dad nods. "Interesting."

"Yep."

"But he's not an artist?"

"So? All my friends don't need to be artists."

"Of course not. But I never thought you'd fall for some jock."

I roll my eyes at him.

Mom finds me in the driveway. "Let's go shopping."

"Okay. What are you looking for?"

"Not for me. For you. You could use some new clothes."

Maybe she wants to bond.

"I saw cute skirts at the mall the other day." My mom walks the mall during the day sometimes, for exercise.

"You think I should be wearing skirts? No one wears skirts to school." Except Vanessa.

"You just looked so pretty in your costume. Why not get some new stuff?"

I did look good in the dress. More . . . grown-up.

I'm into this. Makeover.

Only a few other people are shopping in this department, so I pretend it's closed for me, because I'm a superstar.

If Jewel were here, if he were still my Jewel, we'd play out the whole scene. He'd be my paparazzo. Later, we'd laugh over the photos, but I'd keep one and hang it next to my Dove Girl.

As things are, my mom holds up a skinny navy skirt with something shiny—polished shells?—sewn near the bottom. "Cute," I say.

It's odd to discover that your mother is a better shopper than you are, when you're the teenage girl, but it's fine with me.

I go into the dressing room and put on the skirt. Mom grins when I step out. "Oh, Alice," she says. "This is how I picture you."

It feels good to have my mom think I look pretty. "I like it."

I feel like I'm playing dress-up, though. I would never choose this for myself. I'm not sure why Mom pictures me like this.

"I'm going to look around some more," I say.

When I have my jeans back on, I poke among the racks. Mom is over by the accessories.

I like the salesgirl's denim miniskirt. She shows me where it is on the rack and I try it on.

This I love. I look my age, yet more put together. And my legs look good. I go out to find Mom.

I think I might actually be beaming.

"Honey! That's even better."

"You like?"

"I like how confident you look in it. Just like you did

last night." She brushes the hair from my face. "Like I haven't seen you look in a long time."

So she has been noticing me. My feeling weird has shown, even before anything happened or changed between me and Jewel. I haven't been confident. She's right. "Thanks, Mom," I say, and not just for liking the skirt. For finally bringing this up.

I change again and meet Mom at the register. She's holding clingy V-necks in a rainbow of colors. "Those fit tight," I tell her.

"They're sophisticated. Not just plain cotton."

Okay. If my mom wants me to show off my chest, I guess that's all the go-for-it I need. I do have something to show off.

I notice a rack that I don't want to explore with my mother: lingerie. There are even some neon novelty condoms on a little spinner.

Just then someone behind me says, "Alice!"

I turn; it's Mandy. "Hi!" She looks happy to see me.

"Mom, this is Mandy Walker."

They say hello. Mandy says, "What are you getting?"

I show her the skirt and the three V-necks I'm choosing: light blue, red, and black.

"Cute!" she says. "I want to look for some new jeans."

Mom finishes paying for my stuff, takes the bag, and puts her hand on my shoulder. "I'll leave you girls to it! Meet you at the car in an hour?"

She rushes off before I can protest.

"Cool," Mandy says. "I so need a second opinion."

I show her some jeans that I thought looked good. Of course they fit her perfectly.

She checks out the lingerie before paying. It's lacy, delicate stuff. Nothing like the cotton I usually wear. Oh, God. What if things keep going with Simon? And he, like, sees me in my bra? Or less?

"What do you like there?" I ask her.

She holds up a black bra embroidered with soft pink roses, wiggles it around a little. "Ooh-la-la."

"For sure."

She puts it back. "So you're not meeting your mom for a little. Want to grab a coffee?"

"Always."

We get our lattes and find seats at the mall coffee place. "So," she says. "You and Simon looked like you were having fun last night." She raises her eyebrows and lowers them. "Lots of fun."

I'm sure I blush. "He's pretty great."

"Like how great? I mean, in the kissing department? Come on. Girl talk!"

As if I have much to compare him to. "Stop making me blush!"

"Oh, don't kiss and tell, huh?"

I can't believe a cheerleader and I are having this conversation. Is this the kind of friend I can make now?

"Best. Kisser. Ever." There. I said it.

"And it's just kissing?" She sips her latte like we're talking about the weather.

Whoa. "So far." I try to be as casual as she is.

"Not for long, I bet! He seems really into you."

"You know what? I think he is."

"So how far are you gonna go?"

I'm blushing again. "Let's just say, maybe I should go pick up that pretty bra."

"Ooh-la-la."

I sip my latte and she moves on to telling me about gymnastics.

My mind cartwheels when I realize I've got a new friend.

.

.

.

Chapter Twelve

I see Vanessa in homeroom on Monday. She's wearing Jewel's Backstreet Boys T-shirt. The one I found with him at the junk store last year.

She makes sure I see, sitting up straight as I come in. Usually, she's bent over her notebook, drawing weird things, like factory buildings with shoelaces.

I want to rip that T-shirt off her. And then what would I have? Vanessa in her bra and me left gripping half a T-shirt. Not a good idea, especially the Vanessa-in-bra part.

I'm wearing my jeans with the new black V-neck, and I swear there are eyes on me. In the same way that Corrigan's been leering at me.

I keep my arms folded across my chest, both hands grabbing my backpack straps under my armpits as I walk to my desk.

Vanessa turns around in her chair, watching me.

I am on exhibit.

James Dill sits in front of me. Silent James Dill. He turns around and looks at me. I look back. He finally asks, "Simon Murphy?"

I cock my head.

"And that photo guy," he says. "He used to be your best buddy, right? He's going after Vanessa Almond?" He whispers her name like he doesn't know that the whole homeroom is hyper-tuned to our conversation.

"Kinda."

"Where did you come from," he says, and faces the chalkboard. It's not really a question; he knows I've been here all the time.

This guy named after a pickle suddenly finds me interesting.

Welcome to Popular World, I think.

At lunch, I stare at Simon's lips. I know what they feel like now. I know how he moves them. I know their taste.

I drop my pretzel when he reaches for my hand.

He holds it by the fingers.

"I'm having so much fun with you," he says.

"Me too. With you."

I smile at him. He gives my hand a little squeeze. Something is up.

"Corrigan's having a party this weekend. Want to go?"

"Yeah, sure," I say. That will sort of be my big-time social de-virginization.

"And," Simon says, "he asked if we'd want a room."

Whoa. That could be a whole different kind of de-virgining.

Too fast! Too fast! My brain is screaming. I can't go from gazing at neon condoms from afar to actually needing one. I've just started getting used to kissing.

"Um," I say.

Simon's eyes are on his carrot sticks. Notably not on me. What is he thinking?

This is going way faster than I'd expected. But I'm his girlfriend now and people do go there.

What if I'm only a girlfriend until we get there?

"You know?" he asks.

I just kind of nod. What should I do? I know what he means by "want a room." I so don't feel ready. I was a little embarrassed just talking to Mandy about him seeing me in my bra. How to tell him? Will he break up with me? I push my lunch away.

Corrigan and those guys come up behind Simon. "Speak of the devil," I say.

"Coach posted those new plays in the locker room," Corrigan says. "Let's go."

Simon stands, flashes his dimple at me. "We'll talk later."

During English, I doodle. Simon is in every stroke as I fill a page with countless bubbled-up question marks.

I'm kind of mad that Simon brought up the room. Everything was going so well. He said it; we were having fun. Now there's this big thing already.

He did seem . . . weird about it. And he said it was Corrigan's idea. Is it possible that Simon's nervous too?

On my walk home, I notice that the junk shop has changed its window display. It's full of fifties-esque clothing now, and rhinestone sunglasses.

The rain falls. I concentrate on the traffic passing by, its swishing sound. Like waves.

It's an effort to get through the mile home today. Minimal sleep combined with maximal weirdness has rendered me heavy and slow.

At home, I sink into a nap.

I dream that my Dove Girl has come to life. She's speaking to me, but it's all in Catalan. I have a feeling she's trying to tell me where I belong. But I can't understand.

When I wake up, I work on my art assignment: a still life in charcoal. The rain misses me as I sit under a wool blanket on our front porch in the Adirondack chair and study the tree. The middle-of-the-night tree. The first-kiss tree.

I am beginning to form its trunk when I see someone coming down the street. A guy wearing a black jacket with a hood, moving slowly toward my house. For a second, I'm not sure if it's Simon or Jewel.

When he reaches the porch, Simon stands in front of me, dripping.

"You're soaked." I can't believe he's here. This is what I've dreamed of. It's a boyfriendy thing to do, stopping by like this.

He shakes his head like a wet animal. "I wanted to see you."

I close my sketchpad with the charcoal inside holding my page, smudging my work. "Yeah?"

I put the pad on the wooden deck and sit back to look

at him. Before I know it, he's bent over me, kissing me, drizzling rain from his jacket, his face, his hair. I bet this is what it feels like to shower with someone.

The idea of me and Simon naked together upstairs in the shower while my parents are in the dining room, scheming to save the world, makes me laugh. I pull awkwardly away.

He's grinning. "What's funny?"

I consider telling him, but *No! Keep that little fantasy a secret.* "You! You surprised me."

"Ready or not," he says, "here I come."

We kiss again.

The bedroom proposition enters my head and I freeze.

He pulls back and sits down on the porch by my feet, facing me cross-legged. "So."

"I just, um. I was thinking about . . . the party?"

He looks down at his sneakers. Is Simon Murphy nervous? About me?

I have to just say what I think.

How to phrase it? *"I'm a virgin."* (Duh.) *"No funny business."* *"Have you been tested?"*

Oh, wow. What if the proposition was innocent and he just meant a room in which to . . . talk. Party. Like a VIP thing? Yeah, right.

Say something, say something.

He looks at me. "We don't have to."

I swear, my shoulders deflate with relief.

"We don't?"

"Can I tell you something?"

"Of course."

"Corrigan and those guys just like to talk big. It's part of why I like you," he says. "You're separate from all that. It's easier . . . to be myself around you."

I think I really am dreaming. What movie did he steal that line from, about being himself? Then I see his eyes, aimed up at me. He's sincere.

I want to be with him. I want him to keep looking at me like that.

"Who's gonna be at the party, anyway?"

"Oh, you know. The crowd. Plus usually Nicolai Gregory crashes. People like him. He's fun at parties."

"Plus he's the king."

"Yeah. That too." Simon grins again.

I ask what I really want to know. "Is there any chance that his queen will show?"

"Vanessa? He brings her around sometimes, yeah."

I pull my blanket tighter around myself. "Hey, there's no way Vanessa will bring Jewel to Corrigan's, is there?"

"Would he go?"

"Doubtful."

"So. Probably not. But would you want Jewel there?"

"Jewel at Mike Corrigan's for a social event? That's so alternate universe."

"But he hasn't been hanging out with you lately. What's up with that?"

I look into those emerald eyes. "We're both hanging out with new people."

"Is it . . . at all because of me? I don't want to be in the way of you and your friend. Maybe *you* should bring him to the party. It's fine by me."

That's so sweet. So impossible, but so sweet. "I'd rather just go with you."

He takes my hand. We stare at each other for a while. I can hear the rain pinging on the porch roof. I'm cozy in my blanket. So I share it with him.

We jump apart when my mom calls me in for clam chowder. Simon walks off in the rain, my kisses on his lips.

.

.

.

Chapter Thirteen

At lunch, I sit with Simon's friends now. The girls compliment my hair. "Who does your highlights?" asks Mandy.

"No one."

"You do that yourself? What, drugstore box stuff? Brave girl."

"No. Mother Nature did it." *Mother Nature? What kind of freak am I?*

"Natural?" She squeaks. "Whoa."

The guys mainly talk about sports.

"So, Friday night?" Mandy looks at me over cold veggie burgers. "Corrigan's party!" She pulls sesame seeds off her bun. "You're going, right?"

"Yeah, we're going."

Corrigan grins at Simon and I want to puke. Is that about the room thing?

Mandy looks at me. She's looking at me . . . almost like she's . . . jealous? "This party's gonna rock. I'm so glad you're coming."

Mandy's blond streaks make her look like a model, seriously. "Thanks," I say.

"Hey," she says, "want to do a pairs class with Jim?"

I wonder if people think it's weird that we both take glassblowing classes. But who cares?

"Let's set it up."

∾

On Wednesday, Simon picks me up after dinner.

We drive around for a while and decide to park and look at the view of downtown from the little park on Queen Anne Hill. The Space Needle looks truly alien.

I try to concentrate on what I'm seeing. The sense of Simon, so close, makes it difficult.

My favorite part of the view is that you only know that Elliott Bay is down there because it's the absence of buildings, of lights in the nighttime. Darkest blue. You can look from downtown, over that almost-black water, all the way to West Seattle, knowing that between the pieces of land, another world lives. Orcas.

We stand at the fence, Simon's arm around my waist. His fingers press in and out, so lightly. I can't see anything.

"Are there wild octopi down there?" I ask.

"Sure," he says. "Lots."

"Tell me more about the aquarium," I say.

"The sea otters are fun," he says.

"They're cute, huh?"

"And they eat twenty-five percent of their body weight per day. Kind of like Corrigan."

I smile at that. "You're so informed," I say.

"I don't talk about that sea life stuff with everyone, you know."

"Why not?"

"I guess people would think it's weird."

"I don't."

He looks out across the sound. "I know you don't."

The breeze gets chilly. I don't want to go home yet, so I concentrate on not shivering.

"Let's head out," Simon says.

When we get back to the car he unlocks our doors and puts his keys in his pocket. Not in the ignition.

Literally, we steam up the windows.

Our bodies stretch around the stick shift, the empty travel mug. Simon breathes slow and heavy, and I match his rhythm. It feels crazy, making out like this parked on a street in the ritziest neighborhood in town.

We kiss, rocking. He moves his hands under my tank top, just on my back.

I let him slip his hand under my bra. It feels so amazingly good.

How far am I ready to go? How much do I trust him? Right now I think I'd do anything.

I say, "Let's move to the backseat."

He rests his head on my chest, his hair up under my chin.

How to put this? "More comfy." I kiss his cheek. He leans into my neck, nibbles. He lets out a grunt.

That's when I realize. That grunt. I am so not ready to do this. Like an animal. It kind of makes me feel like I could be just any girl, not special; to Simon, is the physical stuff really only just physical?

I can't believe that, for a second, I was forgetting that when you have sex, you're supposed to be in love.

He moves his head to look at me, eyelashes like curtains. "Are you sure?"

Thank you, thank you for asking. No, I am not sure. Of

anything. When he tells me he loves me, and I believe it, maybe that's when I'll be sure.

I just kiss him again. And again.

I guess he gets the point; no one is moving toward the backseat.

For tonight.

I haven't seen much of Jewel since the Bath, even from a distance. In Spanish, he faces the wall. But I do know that he and Vanessa are glued.

I do my best not to think about exactly what body parts might be coming into contact between the two of them.

I have no right to be jealous that Vanessa is with Jewel. I know that. But I thought I broke his heart at the troll.

Now does he even care about me?

Of course, I see Vanessa in art workshop. She's been doing a series of hearts. Not lovey-dovey bubble ones, but anatomic hearts. Organs. With valves. She's painting them onto canvases, every heart a different color.

Is that her way of falling in love?

Today she works in red.

I focus on my Christmas portrait of Mom and Dad. It's their faces against a red background, which represents our kitchen. My mom's nose is too long, so I get to work on fixing it.

I zone out as I create a better world on canvas.

.

.

.

Friday I take my parents' portrait out of my cubby. I ended up making it more impressionistic because I couldn't quite get their faces right. It's done, I decide. Best I can do.

I walk back to my seat. How much do I wish there were a glass studio at school? Working with glass is all I really feel like doing. After just one lesson it feels more exciting to me than anything in the studio. Plus it's not in the studio. It's my own thing.

My mind wanders. It occurs to me that these are probably the stools that were used in the Bloodbath box room. I could be sitting where spaghetti-brains sat.

As I take out my drawing pad to work on the showcase cover, I smile, thinking of being in that room with Simon. The way he kissed me.

I draw an elephant, huge, his trunk raised.

I go into an art trance as I work on filling in the beast's body.

My mind is blissfully blank until the bell rings.

When it does, I walk out into the hall. Jewel stands there, waiting for Vanessa. He doesn't even look at me as I pass.

My brain spins.

I didn't factor in that gaining a boyfriend might mean losing a best friend.

I barely make it to my locker before I start crying. I bend down and root around in the pile of junk at the bottom of my locker, hiding.

I'm wearing my new denim mini and the light blue shirt my mom chose. The top brightens my eyes.

I have no idea how Simon's friends dress for parties. I can imagine some of the girls in clothes they consider rebellious, from Hot Topic in Westlake Center. Every time I go by there, I think it's where quirky, cool things go to die.

Jewel and I joked about that. It started when we saw a *Gremlins* T-shirt hanging in the window, lusted after it, and then saw Christy VanSant, head cheerleader, wearing it under her J.Crew blazer.

At eight o'clock, Simon's honk comes: three short bursts.

"Hey, good-lookin'," he says as I open the car door and climb in.

He's wearing the same outfit as the day at Pike Place Market. The turquoise sweater, Adidas vest, and his best faded jeans.

I wonder if he knows how much I wanted him that day, before I actually had him. If that's why he's wearing it.

"You look good," I tell him as we zip over to Mike's house.

"It's fun when Corrigan's parents skip town," Simon says as he finds a spot for the car.

People I don't recognize stand on Corrigan's small front porch, drinking out of red plastic cups and laughing too loudly.

"Private school," Simon whispers into my hair as we approach. They all seem to know him, waving and even whooping as we approach.

"Who's your girl?" asks a guy wearing a white baseball cap over his buzz cut.

"This is Alice," Simon says.

This is me, I think. I am Simon's girl.

Inside the house, someone props a stereo speaker on a window ledge.

Some rap song thumps onto the porch.

"Woo-hoo!" screams the guy, raising his drink above his head.

"Let's go in." Simon gives my arm a squeeze.

I follow Simon inside. He acts like it's his own place.

I realize that I've never felt as comfortable even at Jewel's house as Simon seems to feel here. And come to think of it, he has a way of owning whatever space he occupies. I guess that's confidence.

Simon heads directly for the kitchen counter, stocked with a variety of alcohol. Every kid in this place, except for Simon and me, must've raided their parents' stash.

I guess I realized that a party at Corrigan's would mean alcohol, but this is really a lot. Simon seems fine with it, though, even excited about it. I've never really had the desire to get drunk.

He hands me a red cup that smells like raspberries and nail polish remover. I step out of my frame. I take a drink.

Simon pours his own cup to the brim and we move to the couch.

I give myself over, drinking up, chatting with strangers about pop music, borrowing lip gloss from Mandy. As she hands me the tube, she says, "What's mine is yours."

I am at this party. I am the life.

I nuzzle into Simon, leaning on his arm, my head against his neck.

We drink and talk some more.

Simon stands up and takes my hand, leads me back to the kitchen. While he's mixing vodka with lemon-lime soda, Mike stumbles in and opens the fridge. "I gotta find some pepperoni!"

"Only Corrigan decides to make pizza during a party where everyone is drinking but no one is eating," says Simon, stirring his concoction. "I gotta pee."

"Get in line!" Mike shouts.

By the time Simon's back from the bathroom, I'm alone in the kitchen and I've finished his green drink. It tasted like melted Popsicle.

I've gone beyond half-drunk. For the first time in my life. My head feels light. I close my eyes and try to get back into myself. I try to drown out the voices, the pumping music, the sway of the crowd.

Simon grabs me by the waist.

It feels too good.

Then I feel like I might vomit.

Simon burps in my ear. I turn around. His eyes are watery. "I'm pretty gone."

"I can see that." We're both drunk. It's a couple of miles from Corrigan's house to mine. I could walk. "You can't drive me home."

Corrigan comes back to the kitchen, takes his pizza out of the oven, and grabs Simon by the elbow. "Shooting pool," he says. "You versus me."

Simon follows him.

He actually leaves me standing there.

I take deep breaths. I could stay; hang with Mandy. But the world is spinning. Simon's not with me. I feel like I'm falling.

I slip out the garage door and start walking. Carefully.

.

.

.

Chapter Fifteen

Saturday I hear the chimes above the front door when my parents leave for a brunch date with Dad's old colleagues. I stay in bed until one.

They know. When I got home last night they were waiting in the kitchen. I was as quick as possible about saying good night but I'm sure they could tell that I wasn't my sober self.

I've never disappointed them like this before. Or myself.

I sit up in bed and look at my Dove Girl.

It's almost like she's sending me a message, instead of our usual thing, which is all about me asking her for help.

I get out of bed and grab my sketchbook from the floor. I sit on the bed. Close my eyes.

Her face is calmness. She's only a few lines and circles. She's barely even there. Nothing weighs her down. She's light. She can fly.

Pencil to paper, I open my eyes and start with the bird, her wings. The angles of the feathers are so simple, but I've never been able to do them exactly before. *Just breathe,* I tell myself. Pencil up and pencil down. Just shapes.

Then I get to the eyes—curved lines with three-quarter circles underneath. The nose, long with only a slight bend. The lips, a straight line surrounded by a heart.

Pencil up, pencil down. Simple.
I've done it. I've copied her.
And I think she's starting to rub off on me.
I need to find my own peace.
Talking to a poster is so not enough.
I need to concentrate on friends who talk back.

The rest of Saturday is filled with cable television and a Nancy Drew book that I found under my bed. Mysteries solved in the span of about two hours. I wish.

Then I lounge on the couch watching guys who remind me of Simon's friends try to win a date by bench-pressing the girl, who wears a bikini and doesn't have tan lines.

The phone rings as contestant number three lifts the girl. Maybe it's Jewel calling to . . . what? Apologize for leaving me to the wolves?

"Hello?"

"Hey." Not Jewel. But I feel a flutter in my middle.

"Hi."

"You said that already." Simon sounds nervous.

"Did I?"

"So, I'm just calling to say I had a good time at the party."

I did too. But I have a hangover.

And what about the way the night ended? That was so *not* fun. Are we going to talk about it? About Simon's being too wasted to take me home? My face feels hot.

"Yeah," I say.

"You left early."

"You remember?" I am harsher than I want to be.

"Of course," he says. "I looked all over for you."

How can I explain the way I felt at that party without him? "Yeah."

Maybe he'll invite me out and we can talk somewhere. I think there's a good band at the Showbox tonight. I could invite him.

"Hey," I say. "Let's get a *Stranger* from the newsstand and check out the shows tonight."

He breathes. Then I hear Corrigan in the background. He's saying something like "Tell your woman you've gotta go!"

Simon coughs. "Actually, I gotta go."

"Oh."

"I'm at Corrigan's still. Crashed here. We're going for burritos."

I picture them, surrounded by empty bottles and who knows what else. "Sounds good."

"Talk to you later."

Somehow that sounds even less promising than *"See ya."*

Most people would be getting grounded right about now.

Maybe a break from Simon would be the right thing.

At dinner, my parents bring it up. Dad looks at me over his pasta and says, "We need to talk about last night."

"I know," I say. I might cry if I say more, and I really don't want to do that right now.

"No more drinking," Mom says. "None!"

"I know. I didn't like it. It felt awful."

"Remember that feeling," Dad says. "Getting drunk is not all right."

It was horrible being drunk, and seeing Simon drunk. It made me feel . . . more alone than ever. Even at a party, I felt . . . invisible, again.

"This is your freebie," Mom says. "Next time we won't be so easy on you."

"I'm done with it. I swear."

If only I could get Simon to make the same promise.

Simon calls after dinner on Sunday. "How was your weekend?"

He's being casual. "Fine. Yours?" I hope he can hear that I'm being short with him.

"After Corrigan's, I worked at the aquarium. Then today we had practice."

"Oh." I pause.

"Something wrong?"

Yes. I'm waiting for him to apologize for the party.

He left me alone. And then he chose burritos with a beefhead over hanging out with me. It didn't feel like . . . what I want in a boyfriend.

I just blurt it out, "At the end of the party and then all the rest of the weekend, I didn't really feel like I was your girlfriend."

His voice sounds thinner. "What are you talking about?"

"You didn't take me home, or make sure I got there,

and my parents . . . then you didn't hang out with me on Saturday or today. What's that about?" I'm trying not to boil.

"I was having fun. It was a party. And the rest of it? I guess . . . I don't know. I . . . feel like maybe I've been too into you."

I fiddle with the magnets on the refrigerator. "How so?"

He lets out a breath. "I just like being around you so much. I want you to be happy. I guess that's part of why I went with Corrigan at the party. I could tell you weren't really into the party anymore, and I didn't want you to get angry."

"I wasn't angry. It was more . . . uncomfortable."

"I didn't know you felt so bad that you'd leave. I feel terrible about that. I'm going to do better. Okay?"

It's a dream come true.

So why don't I feel lucky?

．

．

．

Chapter Sixteen

Monday morning, I reach the scone place and wonder if I have time to grab coffee. I look in the window and see a blue sweatshirt. That's what I notice first. Not Jewel. His hoodie.

Is Vanessa with him?

God. She lives in Ballard. Of course she's not with him before school.

He turns, sipping what I know is a vanilla latte.

He sees me.

We're caught.

There's still three-quarters of a mile to school and we're both headed that way.

He walks out of the shop and I say, "I liked your photos at the art show."

We fall into step together.

"I didn't think you were there," he says.

Yep, spying through the window. Trying to be invisible. "I helped take down the show."

Okay, we're talking. Just two old friends walking and talking. Except for the elephant walking between us.

He drinks from his cup and I tug on my non-ponytailed hair.

"How are your parents?" he asks.

I think about telling him that my mom mentioned our

families doing Thanksgiving together. She frowned when I didn't say anything.

"They're good."

We pass the junk shop and its window is done up in pilgrims. Corn husks everywhere.

"Aliens," Jewel says.

I look at him. "Like in the Shyamalan movie?"

"Yeah."

We watched that movie on DVD during the summer. We argued about the ending, where it turns out that God has been planning everything just right so that the family can beat the aliens. Jewel thought it was too easy, a stupid explanation. I just liked seeing that everyone was okay in the end. Is that how this will turn out, with everything okay in the end?

Jewel looks at me from the corners of his eyes.

Then he smirks. A tiny smirk, but I know what it means.

I'm finished with the art portfolio cover. It's the best I can do with my Picasso Dove Girl. She's still not quite as angelic as the original, of course. And I'm not at all sure what Mr. Smith had in mind when he asked me to do the thing, so I'm nervous as I walk into art workshop.

I'm relieved to see Vanessa's back turned; she's hunched over some new project involving charcoals and a pile of paper clips. Maybe a gray tribute to the way I've destroyed Jewel.

I drop my backpack on a stool at the table farthest from her, pull out the folder with my drawing.

Mr. Smith is over by the sinks, washing a lot of blue acrylic from his fingers.

I walk over and show him.

"Lovely," he says.

I smile at him.

"Picasso," he says.

"Yeah, my favorite."

"Not Alice."

Well, I did it myself. I colored the eyes green, when Picasso's are empty circles. It's a study. Right?

"I guess not," I say.

"I'd rather see your own mind on the page."

The Dove Girl is my mind. I mean she's on my mind. She's like I want to be. Peaceful. Beautiful. She's alone but she doesn't seem to want anything.

"Give me more of Alice," he says before he walks to his desk.

I would if I could! I want to shout. If I knew who that was. *If you're a fish, you can breathe underwater. If you're Alice, what can you do?*

Simon's at my locker after eighth period.

He grabs hold of my hand as soon as I'm within reach.

He kisses me, there in the hall. The last thing I see before closing my eyes to surrender is Señora Rodriguez walking down the hall with her turquoise rings up near her mouth in apparent surprise at me falling into Simon's arms.

We pull away. I look down at my hand in his and say, "I sort of need that to get my locker open."

He drops my hand. "I'll take you home."

But there's something stopping me. I need to admit it to myself. Something's wrong. He's Simon, and he's fun, and he's a good boyfriend, but he's not . . . he's not my match. The thought makes me a little panicky. *Stop thinking!* But I can't help going on.

Maybe I could've had true happiness and all that with Jewel. Maybe I should've admitted that to myself earlier. Instead of worrying about who I'd dance with in my perfect make-believe dress.

That's not what happened. I'm standing at my locker with Simon and he wants to walk me home.

So I go. I let him feel me up under the tree.

He kisses me, gulping.

I find a note from my mom on the fridge when I get inside, saying, "We'll be at the library late—you're on your own for dinner."

I settle in under the chenille blanket to watch the Horror Channel. It's Japan Week. The movies are totally creepy and the subtitles max the creepiness. Like it's a cartoon or something; like you have to read the words because all that's coming out of the characters' actual mouths is blips. The blips are Japanese, of course, but to me they might as well be exclamation points and stars.

In the movie, a girl is being haunted by a ghost in her new house. The ghost is a milky-white blur. The girl hides under her bedcovers and I drift to sleep myself.

When I wake up, the girl is strapped to a hospital bed

and the ghost is lurking just outside the door, watching her, somehow having traveled with her from the house.

She's the only one who sees it.

My phone rings.

Simon.

"Let's meet up for *pho*. Have you ever tried it?"

"Nope." I try to shake off my nap.

"It's super-good. Noodles and broth and whatever meat you want. Perfect for a rainy night. And they give you a free cream puff."

Macho Simon is interested in cream puffs?

The place is in Ballard. "I'll pick you up." He clicks off.

Didn't I just see him, like, two hours ago?

I leave a note for Mom and Dad, sniff my underarms to make sure they're okay.

I think about changing into my denim mini, but my old jeans feel so comfy.

In the bathroom mirror, I see me looking as good as I ever have. I see Simon Murphy's girlfriend. But she's mad at him. I open the vanity drawer, dig around for an elastic, and put my hair back into its old ponytail.

"Can we stop at Rain City?" I say as I sit down in the car.

"Sure."

Simon parks at Rain City and gets out first, comes around to my side to open the door for me.

Chivalry.

I flash back to the way Jewel and I would joke in the junk shop about being an old married couple. He dug through shoeboxes full of old greeting cards and secretly slipped valentines from the 1950s into my purse for me to find later. He called me honeybunch.

Somehow, that felt more real than this moment with Simon opening my door and ushering me into Rain City. It's not the first time I've felt that Simon and I are in a movie.

"Darling!" Tommy calls from over by the comedies.

He rushes to us and kisses both of my cheeks, Euro-style.

"Who's your friend?" he asks, I'm sure knowing full well who this is from whatever Jewel told him.

"This is Simon."

"Nice to meet you." Simon sounds as if he's meeting my father.

"Likewise, I'm sure."

"So," I say. "I was wondering if you have what's on the Horror Channel right now. I think it's called *Spirit.*"

Tommy goes to check his computer. Simon looks at the new releases and asks if I've seen something with over-grown frat boys on the cover.

Before I answer, Tommy says, "I'll have to order that movie." He blows me a kiss and returns to shelving videos.

Simon gives me a look, all raised eyebrows.

"What?" I ask.

"Nothing." His eyes are aimed toward Tommy's back.

He takes my arm, the same fancy way that Jewel did on that night at the Showbox. Then it made me feel safe. Now I feel . . . like an actress.

At the *pho* restaurant, Simon is talking about his friends. Football. Who wants to hook up with which cheerleader. Apparently, Mike Corrigan has his eye on Molly from Spanish class. He wants to throw another party to try to get in her pants. Something like that.

"Oh my God." Simon puts down his Coke. "Did you hear about this? Corrigan wants to get a Udub tattoo. Purple and gold."

"Yeah?" I ask, sipping my soup.

"The only thing he's not sure of is if he should wait and see if he ends up in a frat, 'cause then he says he'd get the frat's letters instead," Simon says. "Anyway, he's gonna be eighteen pretty soon, so he's up for it."

"What would you get, if you were getting a tattoo?"

"Huh. Maybe a giant octopus, I guess."

I know just what tattoo I'd get.

"I'd get my Dove Girl."

He puts down his spoon. "Your what?"

I never told him about my poster. How could I be thinking I was getting close to someone and not tell him about my Dove Girl?

"It's too strange," I say. "Forget I mentioned it."

"No, come on. I tell you strange stuff sometimes."

"Maybe another time," I say.

He exhales audibly. "What's wrong with right now?"

"Why are you pressing this?"

"Because. I want to know you." His eyes are laser beams.

"You do know me."

"I know *about* you."

"Sorry if that's not enough," I say. What is *wrong* with me? Am I ruining everything? I get up to pay at the register, feeling lousy.

On the sidewalk, I touch his arm. "I'm in a bad mood. I should apologize."

"You should apologize or you are apologizing?" he says. "Don't think so much."

"I'm sorry."

We walk to the car without meeting eyes. When we get to my house, I open the door and get out as soon as the car stops.

.

.

.

It's Saturday again, and my second busy one in a row. Mandy and I set up our glassblowing class for today; tonight there's a party at one of the private school kids' houses. I don't know the guy, obviously, but I'm getting a ride with Mandy and meeting Simon there.

I don't even shower before I head to Fire Art. I'm just going to get all sweaty anyway.

Mandy's waiting outside.

"Hey, *chica*," she says as I approach. "Ready?"

"Can't wait."

Jim is ready. The room's heated up. He hands me a blowpipe and watches as I carry it to the furnace and gather the molten glass. "It's like picking up honey with your finger," I say.

"Except at two thousand degrees," Jim says.

"Yeah, except for that."

And the lesson begins.

I'm in the zone as Jim yells out directions. In the end, my piece is very lopsided, but it'll look cool that way.

"You're getting comfortable with this. I can tell," Jim says as I get ready to leave.

"I love it," I tell him. "Even if I suck."

"At first, no one is good."

Okay, Yoda.

Mandy's been doing her own thing. I almost forgot she was there.

"Wow," I say as she puts her work away. "I was so in a zone."

"Me too," she says, wiping sweat from her forehead. "I thought that only happened to me in gymnastics. Cool."

"Definitely."

"So, I'll see you tonight for the party?" She wipes more sweat, motions to the front door.

I have an idea. Maybe it's about time I had something pretty under my new T-shirt. Maybe tonight Simon and I will fix our little fight; the party will be a good chance to make up. "Hey, why don't we each go home and shower and then meet up to go shopping before the party?"

"Shopping? For a certain something?" She raises her eyebrows at me in that way she did when we were talking about the black bra. "Yay! And bring your party clothes. We can get ready at my house after."

So I'm hanging out with my new friend before the party.

We meet up at the bus stop by Ladro and take the 28 to Pacific Place, back to the store where I went with my mom.

"Here we are," says Mandy, heading straight for the lingerie rack. It's fun having a girl to do this with. She picks up the black number to try on for herself.

She gets me the black one and a pretty purple one. "Try these."

In the dressing room, both bras make me feel like a pinup girl. I've never been so nicely . . . supported.

They're not cheap, but I have enough.

I find Mandy in the front of the store. "I'm getting it, are you?" she asks.

"Yep." I grin. It crosses my mind that she doesn't have anyone special to show it off for. "If it's okay to ask . . . who are you planning to impress?"

She smiles. "It's not about some boy. I just like to feel pretty."

"That's cool."

"Plus, you never know." She grabs a pink bra in her size.

My gaze falls to the neon novelty condoms that are also on the rack. She follows my eyes.

"Not me!" she says.

Phew. "Not me, either. Not yet."

"You and Simon aren't there, are you?"

I think about it. "We probably . . . could be. But. No." Something always holds me back.

"Only do it if you really, really want to," she says. "Some of my friends have been so destroyed by sex with the wrong guy."

"I hear ya."

We go to the register, pay, and head back to the bus stop.

At Mandy's house, no one's home, and we go straight up to her room.

It's like a sanctuary in pink, kind of like a little girl's room, which surprises me. The bed is made. Mine never is.

"Let's do your makeup first," she says. "Then mine."

"Sure."

She has a vanity in her room. Something I've definitely never seen before. I sit on the white-cushioned chair and she gets to work on my face.

Mandy does makeup like a pro, swiftly and with concentration. She has an artillery of brushes.

When she's done, I stare at the mirror and see my eyes brighter than usual, my lips more pouty. It's almost like seeing myself in the witch dress for the first time. "Thank you so much."

"You're welcome," she says. "And you're hot!"

It's seven o'clock by the time we finish getting dressed.

"Pizza?" Mandy asks. "I'm starving."

"Me too. Definitely pizza."

I'm supposed to meet Simon at the party at eight. We have just about enough time.

We take Mandy's car to Mad Pizza so we can go straight from there.

We get to chatting about glassblowing and school, and we don't leave Mad Pizza till eight-thirty.

The party's in Ballard, so we arrive at about eight-forty-five. I figure Simon knows so many people, he probably won't even notice that I'm late.

It's a crazy scene at the party. People I don't recognize are dancing in the living room, with all the furniture pushed to the walls. It's so loud, I barely hear Mandy when she screams "Bathroom!" in my ear.

I feel instantly tense as I push my way through the

crowd, looking for Simon. Some random guy puts his hand on the small of my back. It feels creepy.

Simon's on a kitchen stool. He's drinking a can of cheap beer. He sees me but doesn't smile. "Where were you?"

"I was with Mandy. We got caught up having dinner. I'm sorry. I didn't think you'd mind if I was a little late."

"Wouldn't mind?" he asks. "I've been waiting for you."

Simon was waiting for me? That's sweet. Somehow I imagined that he doesn't think about me much when I'm not right in front of him.

"It's too loud!" I say.

He nods, stands, takes my hand.

We go upstairs and find an empty bedroom. Switch on the light.

"Sorry," I say, keeping Simon's hand. "I just don't really like big crowds like that."

"Now it's just you and me," he says, rubbing my palm with his fingers.

"I didn't mean to be late."

He grabs me by the waist. "Forgiven."

I've heard about guys getting octopus arms in these situations, eight instead of two, but I've never known what it felt like until this moment.

He is everywhere on my body at once as we kiss.

I move my hands up and down his back, slip my hands under his sweater, and he takes this cue to ease my top over my head.

I'm so glad I'm wearing the black bra.

Somehow, though, I am apart from this scene. I am not in it. I feel what Simon is doing and my body responds, but part of me is above, thinking, *This is what it's like to really go at it,* and all I can see is what someone watching us would see.

It's exciting; I like it. But it's weird; it's kind of funny. And I can't stop thinking: Am I doing this just because I want him for my boyfriend? What about love?

"What's wrong?" he asks.

"I'm thinking."

"We'll stop. It's okay." He understands. "This is as far as we go tonight. Just this."

We keep going. I'm melting. His body there on top of mine, skin on skin. How will I ever want this to stop?

Then he pulls away. "If we don't stop now, I don't think I'll be able to."

Exactly.

We breathe there on the bed for a while, next to each other.

"Simon," I say. "Thanks. You're a really, really good guy."

I stand and find my shirt on the floor.

He sits on the bed, pulls on his sweater.

"We're gonna have to wait a minute." I know what he means. His, um, parts, were certainly ready for one of those neon condoms.

"Come sit next to me," he says. He puts his arm around my waist, nuzzles his head against mine, breathes hard.

"Thanks for being so understanding," I say. "I wish . . ." What? I'm not sure what I want to say.

This is real. It's real that I could have sex right now.

Simon just breathes there.

He's not saying anything. Not trying to make me do anything.

Which makes me almost want to do it.

Back downstairs, I spot Mandy on the dance floor with a tall blond guy. She looks happy, jumping around.

Simon goes back to the kitchen and gets another beer out of the fridge. He hands me one.

I think about the last time I drank. "No, thanks. I'm okay."

He widens his eyes at me. "No? It's a party."

"I don't want to today."

Does he think I'm lame for not drinking? "Suit yourself," he says, but his voice is kind of . . . tight.

He finishes his beer fast and goes for another. "Sure you don't want one?"

"I'm sure."

"I thought we were having fun tonight. First you're late. Now you're being . . ."

"Being what?"

"Whatever."

"Just forget about it," I say. The close mood of upstairs has disappeared. "I'm not really into . . . this party."

"Rather be off with someone else? Sorry I'm not *artistic* enough for you."

"What? That's not what I mean! Simon–?" He must be getting drunk. This came out of nowhere. "Excuse me? Did what happened upstairs just happen? It was so nice. I thought that was you up there. My . . . boyfriend. The guy I like."

He stares straight at my eyes. "I thought so too."

I'm beginning to feel like we've gone off script. This is not a happy ending.

Mandy finds me a little while later, after I've escaped to the bathroom and then wandered out onto the back porch.

"Ready, *chica*?"

"So ready," I say.

We pass Simon on our way out, in the middle of the dance floor. Girls are dancing near him, but I don't think any are really dancing *with* him. I fight my way through the crowd and grab his shoulder. "Talk to you tomorrow!" I scream.

He nods but never stops dancing.

I spend Sunday on my own around the house, quiet.

What on earth happened last night? I can't figure it out.

The phone doesn't ring at all, and I barely get off the couch.

Is this life out of my cocoon? Is this what I wanted?

.

.

.

Chapter Eighteen

I walk to school on Monday in a kind of daze. I feel the rain on me and I shiver somewhere deep into my middle, but I'm also on some other planet.

It's like I've started to molt.

Out of my old skin, growing my new.

I left late this morning, to decrease my chances of running into Jewel again. We managed a conversation the other day, but if I talked to him now, I'd be weird. I'd be the girl who wants her best friend back. I'd be the dramatic girl in mourning over the loss of childhood. I'd be mute.

Simon's at my locker.

I walk over, say nothing, and wham, he's got me up against the row of metal.

When we come up for air, he says, "Sorry about Saturday."

"Me too."

But I know it's not all okay. Something won't let me let him in.

I sit in Spanish class with Simon, trying not to watch Jewel in his group with Vanessa.

I sneak a peek at Jewel and he's looking out the window. I guess he's watching the rain.

We used to joke about counting raindrops, trying to say the biggest numbers in our heads. Googolplexes.

After class, Simon rushes out to a student council meeting. Vanessa goes to talk to Señora Rodriguez.

Jewel passes me, keeping three desks away. I say, "Hey." I have to take this chance. If I fall apart, maybe he'll put me back together.

"Hey," he says. He looks at me. Not past me. It's like there's a spotlight again. Like, big moment. Like we should have a billboard.

"Headed home?" I ask. Vanessa is just past his shoulder, but he doesn't seem worried about her. He's over here talking to me.

He nods and we fall into step together.

"Jewel," I say. We're close to home, but I sit down on the wet curb.

He sits next to me and waits for me to go on. I do. "Remember the Charm of Hummingbirds show? Why do you think Simon stood with us? Instead of Corrigan and them?"

Jewel thinks for a minute. "I don't pretend to understand the mind of the masses, but if I had to guess, I'd say it's because you're gorgeous."

I blush.

Now if only I can stop the warmth on my body from Jewel calling me gorgeous. I smirk like he does, trying to hide a huge smile.

That night, my parents have people coming over for dinner. Dad's cooking organic chicken with rosemary, and garlic mashed potatoes.

I help Mom set the table.

She's humming as she brings out wineglasses.

"Mom," I say. "We should invite Jewel and Brenda for Thanksgiving."

She puts down the glasses, smiles at me. "Sounds great."

She comes over and we hug. Just that connection comforts me.

The doorbell rings. The house fills quickly with company chatter as I get my dinner, eat on the porch, and go upstairs.

I lie in bed and look at my Dove Girl.

It's time for things to even out, I think at her. I've been on a teeter-totter.

Simon, up. Jewel, down. Me, up. Vanessa, please stay down. Jewel, up. Would that make Simon go down? I mean descend.

I remember the game Jewel and I used to play as kids, at that park near school. The one where Simon and I went before the Bath.

We used to sit on the teeter-totter's edges and then move forward until we had it balanced in midair. Gentle sway, both of us off the ground, floating. We'd put our feet in front of us and the only thing keeping us up would be that wooden board with chipped paint laid across a rusted metal bar. We could've spent whole days like that.

Simon's big. If we got on a teeter-totter he'd hit the ground and I'd slide down right into him.

.

.

.

Chapter Nineteen

Late for bio already, I stop in the bathroom by the gym.

Someone's crying in a stall.

My first reaction is to head right back out the door.

I'm intruding.

But I've got to pee.

The girl flushes the toilet.

I head into a stall, do what I came in here to do.

Sitting there, I see boots walking toward the sinks.

Vanessa's motorcycle boots.

I want to sit here all day, in the smelly gym bathroom, rather than face her.

But I can't be late for bio.

What was she crying about?

I count to ten by Mississippis, waiting for her to wash up and get a move on.

I can still see her boots shuffling around near the sink.

I am officially late for bio.

I head out to the sinks.

For one moment I wish I could be as invisible as I used to feel.

Vanessa is leaning over one of the filthy sinks, applying eyeliner.

She flinches when she sees me coming up to wash my hands at the other sink.

"Damn allergies," she says. "My eyes water."

I give her a half-smile. "I hate when that happens."

"Yeah, well"—she caps her eyeliner—"it's really none of your business."

She brushes by me.

The rumor mill at school is churning.

In the cafeteria Mike Corrigan shouts over at me, "Hey, Alice, your bud and Vanessa are over. I heard it from that Amber chick during trig."

Simon gives me a look.

"That's interesting." My brain floods. When did this happen? And why?

I'm napping when my mom wakes me up. I smell beef stew cooking downstairs. I roll over and say, "Dinnertime!"

"Honey, Jewel's here to see you."

It's a good thing I just woke up. Otherwise, I'm sure my face would show that I feel like one of those cartoon Acme anvils has just been dropped on my head. I am Bugs Bunny befuddled.

"I'll send him up," she says.

I sit, still covered in my blanket, and look at my Dove Girl. *Help!*

He's on my window seat, just looking at me. He doesn't seem nervous at all. When he's nervous, his eyes look behind you, not at you. Like at the troll that day. He studied the VW instead of looking at my eyes. He was mad and he didn't know what to say and I'm sure his heart was like a hammer hitting a nail and hitting it and hitting it.

Now he's different. Aside from looking at my eyes, he's also got messy hair. For Jewel, messy hair is usually an art. He uses mousse, although he'd die of embarrassment if people knew that. Today he's frizzy.

Is he jumbled over Vanessa? Or what?

"Vanessa likes you, you know," he says. "She's jealous of you sometimes."

This is the last thing I expected to hear. I think about it. *Likes* me? She can be kind of mean to me sometimes, like when she almost dripped paint on my work that day in the studio. But I can see it, I guess. We're too similar, really, to not like each other. Even if we might drive each other insane.

I look at Jewel. "She's so out there."

"Because she's insecure."

I try not to seem surprised. Instead, I pick at the bedspread. Could that be?

Once you start looking at someone like they're a real person, it's easy to see that something's going on under the surface.

Jewel fidgets. "I broke up with her."

"I know." Crying in the girls' room is not a sign of being a dumper; it was about Vanessa being the dumpee.

He's silent. Closes his eyes. Opens them. "You know you'll always be the most important person to me."

At that, my heart leaps.

And then I understand what else he's saying.

"And that's why you broke up with Vanessa?"

He stands up. "Yes."

I watch him leave my room and hear him pound down the stairs in his Jewel way. I want so badly to follow him.

Now I know. I know I have to undo everything with Simon.

Simon's decided to take me for a picnic on Sunday night.

Here's my opportunity. I can't be with him anymore. It's not right. I'm not ready for something so big. I have to say those words.

If only I weren't still so, so attracted to him. There are a lot of good things about Simon. A lot that I'll miss. Like holding on to him. Looking into his eyes. His voice. Kissing him.

Aside from lust . . . he's basically a good person. He makes me feel wanted. Sometimes he makes me feel I'm special. He showed me something important about how to be social. He opened doors for me.

Now I have to close a door for him. An Alice-sized door.

Even if we had a fight, I don't think he's expecting me to say I'm done.

How am I going to do it?

We get bundled up and head to Golden Gardens, wind chilling us.

We spread out a blanket he brought and sip red wine he snuck from his kitchen out of plastic cups. His arm is around me.

"Are you cold?" he asks, and I nod before I can think.

He stands, takes my hand, wraps the blanket around my shoulders, and leads me to his dad's car in the parking lot.

When we get there, he opens the front door for me.

Then he takes the blanket and opens the back door, spreading it on the backseat. "In case we want to get comfortable."

Who knows what we might do back there? Except, I know. Nothing is going to happen. Nothing but me breaking up with my first boyfriend. But *how*?

He comes around to the driver's side and slides in next to me.

I'm taking the tiniest sips of wine, like Jewel with his first latte that time when we were twelve. I'm only pretending to drink it. I'm only pretending to like this.

The beach is like a film with smells. Seaweedy. Fishy. Lights from across the bay reflecting off the gently pulsing water.

Simon's hand on my knee is fire. I look at him and I can tell I look good.

He tosses his empty cup on the floor.

I worry about it getting caught under the brake pedal when he drives me home in a few minutes.

He takes my cup, sets it on the dash.

I never wanted to be getting it on in some car.

I never wanted to be drinking to get myself there.

"Come here," he says.

How do I say this?

"Simon, I . . . I need to go home."

He looks at me.

I can't face his eyes. I look at the dashboard.

How can I explain that I'm not this girl now? That I need something else? That I had a great time with him, but he's not . . . who I need? I'm not ready to be his girlfriend. Or anyone's.

He's listening. "Simon . . . you're . . . amazing. When we fool around, I love that. I do. I'm sure you know. God . . . the way you kiss."

He squeezes my hand. "So what's the problem?"

"It's . . . I like . . . how you see me. I thought I was invisible before you."

"No way. I wanted to talk to you for so long before we ever did."

"I didn't know that."

"It's true."

"I believe it now."

He's still holding my hand, stroking it with his thumb.

"What I didn't realize is that having a boyfriend isn't enough to make me . . ."

"Yeah?"

"I don't know. It's like I'm always trying to figure out how to be comfortable with myself. And dating you has been amazing and I've loved it. Which is good. Which is what I wanted a month ago. But I still don't feel . . . right."

"But what did I do?" His thumb is still.

"You did everything right. You're amazing."

"So . . ."

"It's just about feelings that are . . . hard to explain. Like I hesitated to tell you about my Dove Girl."

"I guess I've noticed that you don't always let me in. That's why I thought I was the one more into it. But things seemed okay after we talked on the phone after Corrigan's party."

"She's a poster."

"The Dove Girl?"

"She's who I talk to. She's like my symbol of peace. I talk to her because I don't think I have anyone else to talk to."

"That's crazy. You've got . . ."

"Jewel."

"And me."

"I did. But now I realize that I can't force it. The connection, I mean. I had a crush on you. A huge crush."

"So . . ."

"I'm just not melting with you anymore. I'm not . . . ready. Or something."

He's silent for a full minute. "Melting? Alice." He looks at me. "You've been kind of . . . my best friend lately." His eyes start to water. "I meant it when I said I'm not into the whole football scene. I'm . . . I want to keep seeing you."

I'm tempted to touch his cheek. But I can stop that impulse. I can resist him; that's the problem. I'm being pulled another way.

"I wish I could be what you want, Simon. I really do. But I just . . . I just can't."

Then he drops my hand.

I know that was the last time.

.

.

.

Chapter Twenty

The weirdest part of Monday is art workshop. Vanessa smiles at me as soon as I walk in the door.

It's not her usual thing either. The smile's somehow sympathetic.

We could be a photo. Vanessa with that smile, me with a mirror image.

Girls bonded by broken hearts.

Even if I'm the one who ended things with Simon, my heart *is* a little broken. I'm back to being alone. At least, that's what I think when I feel insecure. Then I tell myself I have a new chance with Jewel, a new friend in Mandy, and maybe even . . . a nonenemy in Vanessa.

I'm deep inside my sweatshirt hood, hoping Mr. Smith will realize I don't feel like being talked to.

I haven't finished the new art portfolio cover yet.

Okay, I haven't even thought of an idea for it.

My sketchpad is in front of me, open to the first blank page. The page after my last, best attempt at my Dove Girl.

I need to do something new. Absolutely.

Mr. Smith wants more Alice in my work.

If I close my eyes, I can see colors swirling on my closed lids. Shapes that pulse, glide, and fade. I can see glass, heating and cooling.

I see a series of tiny glass globes. What colors? I'll ask Jim when I can start learning to add color.

I slip my hood down and begin to draw.

Vanessa's watching from across the room, always watching when I talk to Mr. Smith.

Her latest work is clay sculptures of tiny animals. They're beautiful.

Mr. Smith is working with the letterpress.

"I don't want to do the portfolio cover," I tell him. "I'm just not really into it. I've got some good ideas for other things."

He runs his fingers through his hair, the way he does when he realizes that he's a teacher and not just an artist who happens to work in a school.

"Let Vanessa do it," I say. "She'll do a better job."

I walk home alone. The rain is heavier than usual and I can hear it pinging my hood. I'll have to change my jeans when I get home.

Just as I'm passing John, the homeless guy, sitting outside Caffe Ladro getting soaked, Jewel comes up beside me.

He doesn't say anything.

We walk a whole block with both of us looking down at our sneakers.

"Troll?" he says, and I follow.

It's drier up by the troll, under his bridge. I take down my hood.

"Hey, your ponytail's back."

For just a second, it's like we've stepped back in time, to another day at the troll. Maybe even to our kiss day. The graffiti on the VW is gone now; the troll's back to normal.

I take three steps to cover the distance between us and sink into a Jewel-hug. I tingle. That old tingle. Should I act on it? Should I kiss Jewel?

No. I just want to be friends again, at least for a while. His hands feel strong. He smells so good, familiar. That's what I really need.

"It feels great to be friends again," I say. "I never stopped feeling like you're my best friend."

"You said the F-word."

Oh, no. Is he going to explode because I only want to be friends?

He narrows his eyes. "I'll accept that for now."

We climb up the troll's back and sit.

The news of me hooking up with Simon and Jewel hooking up with Vanessa was huge.

My reunion with Jewel is nothing.

Only, it's everything.

When Vanessa sees me in art workshop the next day, she kind of smiles, but her eyes look sad.

She doesn't roll her eyes anymore.

She closes them.

☙

Jewel and I are halfway through root beer floats with chocolate syrup when I shift on my kitchen chair and tell him what I think. "Vanessa really misses you."

It's not until then that I realize that Jewel and I have totally avoided the subject of Vanessa.

"I know," he says. "Because of the string."

I chew on my straw, waiting for him to explain.

"She wears strings around her wrist."

"Yeah," I say. "I've noticed that. Never really thought about it."

"It's a cool idea, actually." He sips his float. "They're color-coded depending on her mood."

"Oh, so like red might be 'happy.' "

" 'Happy' is purple, but yeah."

"So, what? She's been wearing something bad?"

He sucks the dregs of his float before answering.

"Black."

"Bad."

"It's the worst."

That night, the phone rings. "Hi."

"Mandy?"

"Hey, *chica*."

"Hey." I picture her sitting on her pink bed with fluffy covers.

"So you and Simon are over?"

It's nice of her to call.

"Yeah."

"I just wanted to say that, you know, you could still sit with us at lunch."

"Thanks," I say. "That's really sweet. But I don't think I want to be around Simon for a while."

"Oh!" She sounds surprised. "I didn't mean *that* us. I'm so over those boys, with all their macho-macho stuff. Do you know Corrigan expected me to let him go under my skirt at that party last Saturday? We're not even dating. I'm just supposed to be in awe of his football-hero thing because I'm a cheerleader."

"Eew. Somehow I'm not surprised. But eew."

"Yeah, so I just mean me and my girls. For lunch."

"That sounds great."

In Spanish, I see Simon. "Hey." I smile at him.

"Hi." He nods. It's weird how so much can turn into so little.

Luckily Señora Rodriguez announces that we're switching conversation groups today.

My new group: two sophomore friends of Molly's, and Vanessa.

She's sitting right in front of me, that black string tied around her wrist. Double-knotted.

In our books we've moved on from colors to foods.

The *"yo quiero Taco Bell"* jokes are never-ending and Molly's two friends are two of the biggest perpetrators.

"Taquito!"

Pink fingernails tapping on the desk.

"*Gordito!*"

Cackle.

"*Muchos nachos!*"

Vanessa winces.

"Um," I say. "Let's do breakfast. *Yo quiero a comer huevos.* I want to eat eggs."

Vanessa and I are both good in this class. Really good.

So I get it when she tells me in Spanish that what she wants to do with the *huevos* is crack them in the loud girls' pretty hair.

My turn to cackle.

Vanessa approaches me at my locker, almost smiling. She's holding a paper lunch sack. The string around her wrist is blue.

She hands the sack to me. "Open that."

It's a white dove, clay.

"I hope you like it," she says. "Jewel told me a couple times about your poster."

"Wow," I say, holding it carefully. What a present!

I love it. She gets me. Vanessa *is* someone I could be friends with. Who knew?

"You're not mad, are you?" she asks. "I know it's private, but Jewel only told me 'cause he thought it was cool. I think it is too."

"Mad? No way. This is . . . lovely. Thanks."

∾

Now that I'm out of my cocoon, and past being a girl-friend, I'm just me, finding my way through the halls. Eating lunch with Mandy and her friends. Talking about art with Vanessa. Doing what I do.

Friday at the end of *la clase de español,* Simon's off to football practice without a glance in my direction. Vanessa's headed to put some finishing touches on something in the art studio. Otherwise, maybe we'd hang out after school today. We're about at that point.

After she walks away down the hall, Jewel appears right behind me.

I turn around. "Let's go get a movie."

So my best friend and I head home.

On the way, I feel static between our bodies. Maybe we're just getting used to each other again. Maybe we're charged with some new feelings.

Does he still want to kiss me? The idea makes me smile. I might soon decide to attack him with my own kisses.

But for now, just walking to Rain City is enough.

I reach out and take Jewel's hand.

Acknowledgments

.

.

.

Thank you, thank you, thank you, to . . .

Wendy Lamb and her team at Random House: Ruth Homberg, Robert Warren, Kaitlin McCafferty, Andrew Bast, and Katie Harmon.

Rosemary Stimola, Miracle Agent.

My Vermont College advisors: Lisa Jahn-Clough, Ron Koertge, Tobin Anderson, and Cynthia Leitich-Smith. What a lineup. What a dream come true.

The Vermont College MFA in Writing for Children and Young Adults faculty, and my VC friends—especially my lovely classmates.

Anita Silvey, for the scholarship and for her enthusiasm.

Lara Zeises, unofficial mentor in all things YA.

The staff at All for Kids Books & Music, where YA literature is loved and understood.

My family and friends, who have been eternally patient in waiting to read this novel. Glad it's finally in your hands.

Thanks to Random House for helping me try to find a permissions source so that we could use an image of Alice's Dove Girl in this book. Sadly, it was not possible to obtain permission to reproduce that well-known image by Picasso.

About the Author

.

.

.

Liz Gallagher grew up in the suburbs of Philadelphia and
was an English major at Penn State. She worked on the edi-
torial staff of *Highlights for Children*. She is a graduate of the
University of Denver Publishing Institute and the Vermont
College MFA program in writing for children and young
adults. Her home in Seattle is within chomping distance
of the Fremont Troll. This novel is her first, and her dream
come true. Visit her online at www.lizgallagher.com.

∾